T0128335

FREELANCE

For Better or Worse

JOSEPH JOHN SZYMANSKI

FREELANCE
FOR BETTER OR WORSE

iUniverse books may be ordered through booksellers or by contacting:

iUniverse
1663 Liberty Drive
Bloomington, IN 47403
www.iuniverse.com
1-800-Authors (1-800-288-4677)

Because of the dynamic nature of the Internet, any web addresses or links contained in this book may have changed since publication and may no longer be valid. The views expressed in this work are solely those of the author and do not necessarily reflect the views of the publisher, and the publisher hereby disclaims any responsibility for them.

Any people depicted in stock imagery provided by Getty Images are models, and such images are being used for illustrative purposes only. Certain stock imagery © Getty Images.

ISBN: 978-1-6632-0114-0 (sc)
ISBN: 978-1-6632-0115-7 (e)

Print information available on the last page.

iUniverse rev. date: 05/16/2020

Dedication

This novel is dedicated to my late wife, Renate Lippert Szymanski, who was born in Bavaria, the site of this novel. She was my heart and soul from the time I first met her in 1970 in Munich when she was 21 until she died in Pasadena, California in 1986 at the age of 36.

Acknowledgement

Without the encouragement, assistance, and contributions of Muphen Renee Whitney this novel would not have been started and completed. Whatever joy or sadness it brings to the reader, it brings the same effects to the author twice-fold because of the inspiration of Miss Whitney. The author also predicts that the final words of this book, suggested by Miss Whitney, will go down in history for years to come and will be repeated by current and future generations, especially when spoken and written by reporters and commentators around the globe.

The reader is also advised -- i.e., warned -- that every word in this novel is fictitious, which means that all characters, events, dates, and names that appear are fictitious. Any resemblance to individuals living, dead, or in-between is entirely coincidental and unintentional. Anyone alive and able to think and act is better off not being construed as a character in this novel. Remember fiction, like litigation, is good. It works, and when you win it is almost as delicious as *Marie Callender's* apple pie!

Introduction

L ike every good writer of fiction, I have in my heart for this novel alone a favorite hero who is surprisingly not a family member or friend. His name is Buck, a 29-year-old photojournalist from Hoboken, New Jersey. He is foremost honest to an extreme, but he is a rogue -- one who is fearless but never cruel. When he tilts his head slightly to one side, be on guard for he is sizing you up. And never ever try to touch the Stetson or sunglasses that he is wearing.

To know more about him, hop aboard the express train he is taking on his first trip abroad in search of his mother's birthplace in Germany. It all begins with the loud blare of a train air horn...

Chapter 1

It was a bright sunny morning in late September midway between Stuttgart and Munchen in Germany. Before your eyes were a dense forest of Tannenbaums, a river running alongside train tracks, lush meadows with cattle grazing leisurely, and chalets sprinkled haphazardly. This region is known as one of the most picturesque in Germany. It is a photographer's paradise with all of God's embellishments.

Not a sound was heard to the human ear as a white-tailed eagle with its grayish mid-brown plumage and yellow bill, feet, and eyes spotted something familiar. On the horizon three miles away, humans could not spot it with their eyes but for an eagle it was as clear as a white-tailed rabbit suddenly coming into view.

The eagle remained in its upright stance until hunger got the best of it, then it gracefully pushed away from its perch. It climbed to a height of 1,000 feet until it recognized the pale greyish-white, bullet-shaped engine with a bright red line running completely around the train. The eagle's wings extended to a span of seven feet as it glided down and leveled off as Germany's most modern train began to pass by on its right side.

After adjusting to the train's aerodynamic headwind, the eagle relaxed and looked into the oval window of each car as it passed by seemingly in slow motion.

Eventually the restaurant car arrived and the eagle managed to maintain a position alongside the bay window. The eagle opened its bill as if to call out to someone standing inside: a young man dressed in a western shirt, denim jeans, cowboy boots, a Stetson, and sport sunglasses.

"Krau, krau, krau," the eagle called out. "For Krist sakes, why won't those humans pay attention to me? Oh well...Welcome to Germany, folks," he cried as he gracefully flapped his wings and flew off in a high swooping arc.

A high-pitched air horn suddenly blared from the engine of the InterCity Express train as a warning that it was approaching a railroad crossing. The blast sounded just as the steward tending bar inside the restaurant car finished pouring a bottle of beer into a glass for Buck Simon. The 6-foot 3-inch young man pushed his beige Stetson farther above his forehead until his blond hair appeared to have a gold tinge. It matched the golden glow of his Dortmunder Union beer. Then he lowered his Porsche Sport sunglasses until he could peer over them to watch a foam form at the top of his Pilsen glass. He had a taste of the beer, raised the glass high, and took a photograph with the digital camera strapped around his neck.

"Caption for beer aboard the ICE," he said to no one in particular, except his cell phone. "First beer on my first trip abroad. Gold color, probably influenced in brewing by Pilsen in Czechoslovakia, moderate bitterness but packed with flavor thanks to noble hops. I learned a lot about German beers at Lehigh U."

He swallowed the entire beer, slammed his glass down on the bar countertop, and belched loudly enough to draw the ire of passengers nearby. He then grabbed his luggage and weaved through the crowded car, eventually approaching the connecting door of the train. He waved his left hand to break the electronic beam that opened the door until it closed with a loud bang.

Buck walked slowly down the corridor of the adjoining car

and remembered what the conductor told him about finding his compartment. He carefully peered into the top left side of the first window to find the compartment number and seat he had reserved. Although this was not his compartment, he could not resist pausing to admire a beautiful lady with her skirt positioned halfway up her thigh. He thought for a brief moment about barging in accidentally just to see if she might react favorably to his intrusion but hesitated when he thought the odds were against his chances of beginning a worthwhile relationship.

Buck shook his head from side to side and moved further down the corridor, then he spotted a five-foot eight-inch voluptuous girl walking toward him. She looked to be in her mid-20s and was wearing an embroidered dirndl, cut low to reveal a set of knockers that servicemen in olden days referred to as torpedoes.

As she was about to pass him, the slight bend in the tracks caused the train to swerve, forcing her to draw closer and brush up against him. Buck reacted with a big smile and lifted his digital Canon camera high in the air over one shoulder.

"Can you tell me where the restaurant car is on this train?" she asked with an enticing smile.

"It's straight ahead, one more car in the same direction you're headed."

"You just could have told me it was in the next car. Did you prolong your words to take a photograph of my …?"

"Dirndl?" he responded. "I make it a rule never to take a shot without the permission of the persons being photographed. As for you, I had in mind another angle with a close-up of what's inside your beautiful …"

"Why don't you be honest and say breasts?"

"You do see what I am thinking. Just like my camera, you read my mind. I anticipated a close up … of your embroidered bodice."

"You're putting me on … Did you get your shot?"

"I won't know until I have a chance to review the photos," he answered with a devilish grin. "You should know that my camera is

3

a living thing. When aroused, it will go off prematurely, on its own volition. Often uncontrollable. It has a mind all its own."

"I don't believe a word you said. You have a digital camera, don't you? Are you joshing me around?"

"Is joshing something like a roll in the hay?"

"My name is May Bea Forshur. I'm a farmer's daughter from Stuttgart on my way to the Oktoberfest in Munich for a good time. I know a lot about a roll in the hay."

"You can call me Buck, always quick with the buck but no schmuck. As a farmer's daughter, perhaps you can answer something that has puzzled me for a long time."

"If it's about farming, we specialize in growing the juiciest green tomatoes in the state of Baden-Wurttemberg. Our farm is on the Neckar River in the fertile valley known as *Stuttgart Cauldron*."

"Is it true that a farmer's daughter can make a green tomato blush into a sweeter red one by standing nude in front of the vine?"

"Are you kidding? Of course not, but it will affect the cucumbers."

"How?"

"Agriculturally speaking, I haven't a clue. You got me there. Cucs have a mind all their own, and when they see a nude woman, they expand to an enormous length and hardness."

She stopped looking into his eyes and looked at his groin. "There is nothing quite like the feeling I get when wrapping my hands, ah I mean my fingers, around a cuc!"

"Your point is well taken."

"I will take it in hand," she answered with another glance at his groin.

"Really? Well, I don't have a cucumber, but I do have a Canon. Would you like to hold my Canon?"

"Yes, by all means, but at another time and place."

"Your agricultural explanation is very elevating and uplifting, like the perfume you are wearing. It arouses my senses."

"Do you recognize it?"

"Yes, I do. *Shalimar* by Guerlain. It was a favorite of someone very close to me when I was growing up in Hoboken."

"I don't know where Hoboken is, but I now know where the restaurant car is. Would you like to join me for a bite?"

"I don't bite and never have, but right now I need to find my compartment and get organized."

Then Buck looked down at her cleavage and began to salivate. He wondered if he was doing the right thing by not giving in to the appeal of her body.

May Bea took a handkerchief from her purse, wiped Buck's lips, and told him that he was drooling.

Buck licked his lips and told her, "I'll be in touch. Oh, baby, will I be in touch!"

May Bea fanned her face with her hand to cool off this encounter that was full of double entendres. She looked back twice as she strolled out the connecting door to the next car.

Buck watched her every step, especially the way she swung her hips. He fell back against the corridor wall to catch his breath and realized that he didn't get her address or phone number or give her his phone number.

"How stupid am I for not exchanging more information," he said to himself.

In the past he never hesitated when it came to making a play for a beautiful girl. He called it whether or not "to go for it." He admitted that making an advance may lead to his making a complete fool of himself, but it was always fun to see how it played out.

Nonetheless, to make a better-than-average name for himself as a photojournalist, he had to be careful not to be offensive.

Now at this point in the story, I hope that the reader recognizes the attributes of our leading man Buck, a handsome hunk known for his imagination, courage, good sense of humor, persistence, and ingenuity.

Buck took only a few steps before he discovered his compartment. He opened the door, glanced at the four passengers inside, and tossed his luggage in the overhead rack. Then he tipped his Stetson, gave a half-assed salute, and said in a loud voice with a Western twang, "Hallo, Gruss Gott, Guten Morgen, Wie Gehts, Wilkommen, and Howwwwdy!"

At the precise moment that he plopped down in his seat, the compartment turned pitch black, darker than dark, blacker than black, because the train entered a tunnel.

Buck grabbed his camera and scrolled through recently-taken photos to see if he got the shot of May Bea Forshur. He sighed in relief when he found at least three good close-ups appearing on the screen, thanks to the software installed in his digital camera. The camera snapped just the shots Buck wanted.

Buck then turned his head to gaze through the wide picture window. He was temporarily hypnotized by periodic sparks that erupted from the interaction of train wheels onto steel rails. The sparks reflected in shades of blue and white against the rock-lined tunnel and into the walls and ceiling of his compartment. They danced around like fairy lights.

There was no clickety-clack from this sleek bullet-shaped engine – this marvel of engineering whose speed can reach up to 300 kilometers per hour. The train moved as if it were floating on a magnetic cloud.

"The thing about tunnels," Buck said out loud to no one in particular, "is no one but God can predict how long the darkness will last until he says, "Let there be light!"

Suddenly, the morning sun pierced brightly through the window where the other passengers were seated comfortably in their first-class seats. They all seemed to be talking at once as Buck pushed his Stetson further above his forehead and lowered his sunglasses down his nose so he could peer eye-to-eye with his new train mates. He had much to look forward to on his first day in Bavaria.

"You know," said Buck, who paused to draw in a deep breath,

"nothing beats traveling first class, unless it's when your boss picks up the bill."

"What you say might be true," said Rudi Hofstedler, a 45-year-old Philadelphia-based lawyer. "But I prefer to be on my own and not under any obligation to anyone, especially when traveling on a vacation. This is our first trip abroad."

"Well," said Buck, "you certainly chose a perfect time because the Oktoberfest started last Saturday at noon in Munich when the Mayor tapped the first barrel of beer at Schottenhamel Tent, which is more like a giant airport hangar than a tent."

"Have you been there before?" asked the lady sitting next to Rudi; Rudi introduced her as his wife Sylvia.

"No. This is my first trip abroad, too," said Buck. "My mother was born in Bavaria, and I'm on my way to the village outside Munich where she was born. She often raved about the fun she had during Oktoberfest with all its good food and liquid refreshment."

When his fellow passengers indicated an interest in attending the event later in the week, Buck explained in more detail what to expect at Oktoberfest. He told them that the Fest was about 14 days long and would end the first Sunday after October 5th.

"More than six million people will be attending, so reservations are a must if you want a seat inside the hangars sponsored by the best breweries in Germany. On the grounds outside the hangars you will love all the amusement rides, side stalls, games, and a wide variety of traditional food such as grilled fish, rotisserie chicken, and roast pork (otherwise known as schweinebraten and sweinsaxe), kalbsrahmbraten smothered in cream sauce, grilled ham hocks, grilled sausage, potato dumplings, potato pancakes, sauerkraut, and red cabbage."

"Wow, that's a mouthful, I mean the way you expressed it," said Sylvia. "I can't wait to taste them all, one at a time, of course!"

"Oh, I intentionally left the best until last -- the white sausage called Weisswurst," said Buck. "The blend is a secret with butchers, but it basically is made with fresh veal minced with pork back bacon, parsley, lemon, mace, onions, ginger, and cardamom. It's a delicacy throughout Germany. Munich, according to my mother, has the best tasting Weisswurst. After eating two or three, you will feel as though you have died and gone to heaven!"

"I can't wait to try them," said Rudi, "even if they're not kosher."

"Being from Philly," Buck replied to Rudi, "you probably know about *Tastykakes*. Well, my Mom called Weisswurst *Tastylinks* and *Tastywurst*."

His fellow passengers were enthralled by Buck's comments as he leaned back in his seat and continued to tell them that he felt as if he were coming home although this was the first time he would set foot outside America in search of his mother's birthplace, a small village called Fischbachau.

"I had heard much about this area where my mother lived before she married, moved to America, and settled in the Bronx with my father. Then after I was born, my family moved to Frank Sinatra's birthplace."

"Forgive me but you have put me in the dark," said Rudi. "I haven't a clue about where Sinatra was born. Ask me about donations, probates, trusts, and financial planning, and I'll give you the perfect answer."

"Hoboken," said Sylvia.

"Smile when you say that, partner," said Buck, with his western twang, "and add that it's in *New Joysee*."

Sylvia promptly smiled broadly at Buck and nudged her husband gently with her elbow. "I had a huge crush on Frank Sinatra from the first time I heard him sing *Be Careful, It's My Heart*."

"Sing a few bars for these folks, meine schatze," said Rudi, "please."

Sylvia leaned forward a little and began singing slowly with feeling in a voice resembling Jo Stafford.

> *Be careful, it's my heart,*
> *It's not my watch you're holding, it's my heart.*

It's not the note that I sent you that you quickly burned,
It's not a book I lent you that you never returned.
Be Careful, It's My Heart - Frank Sinatra

Rudi faked a move as if to grab an invisible microphone from his wife's hands and continued to sing the song in German.

Denken Sie daran, es ist mein Herz,
Mit dem ich mich bereitwillig teile.

Sylvia faked the same act with the microphone and took a seat next to Buck and sang the last words of the lyric close to his ear.

It's yours to take, to keep or break,
But please, before you start,
Be careful, it's my heart.

Be Careful, It's My Heart - Frank Sinatra

"Obviously, my wife is a flirt, but a kind one," said Rudi, laughing.

"That was *tres jolie*," said one of the attractive 21-year-old twin girls seated by the window across from her sister. "My name is Afta L'Heure."

She moved a wide strand of her red hair that covered her right eye to resemble Veronica Lake, then stretched out her tongue to lick the right side of her lips. It was an action she did from childhood without any reason.

"And I am Beafore L'Heure," said the other twin. "We're identical twins, so they tell us."

She moved a similar strand of her red hair that covered her left eye and stretched out her tongue to lick the left side of her lips. It was an action identical to her older sister, except in the opposite corner of her lips.

"We're also making our first trip abroad, and we loved your interpretation," said Afta.

The twins explained that they were born in the French Quarter of New Orleans to French immigrants. They were so united that they spoke and thought as one, with a decidedly strong southern accent. They were known to finish each other's thoughts and sentences without missing a beat.

Buck's heart began to twitter a bit after scanning their dresses. Both were sporting a cotton dirndl, with a low-cut bodice and short puffy sleeves. Their skirt was simple and plain, a cross between rose and orange in color, tailored with a border of embroidered, hand-woven flowers.

"Where is your apron?" Buck asked. "Just kidding. You both look like living dolls!"

After a brief pause, he added, "I know about dirndls from my mother. She often wore hers for special occasions such as the festivals in Hoboken."

"What brings you to Munich?" Rudi asked the twins.

"We won fellowships to study mural painting at the Munich Academy of Art. Our course will begin in two weeks," said Beafore.

"We thought it would be nice to see the countryside," said Afta, "especially the mountains and lakes around Munich before settling down for a year of rigorous training. We bought these dirndls to wear next week when we visit the Oktoberfest in Munich."

Both twins leaned forward to reveal sizable cleavage for a 21-year-old. Buck predicted how they would stand out at the Fest and how they would have to fight off men eager to have a date with them.

"How and why was your fellowship awarded to both of you?" Rudi asked.

"The State of Louisiana conducted an open contest," said Afta.

"We competed as one entry because we always work together," Beafore said with pride.

"Our paintings of horses are popular with owners and trainers of horses, especially those who have horses with Arabian bloodlines," Afta said.

"We have enjoyed our commercial success," Beafore added, "but now we are so happy to have the feedback and acceptance of the competition's judges."

The twins then thought back to the competition when many artists were hard at work in front of easels in a small rotunda. Their concentration and intensity to compete for a fellowship were evident. The silence while the artists were creating their entries was noteworthy and nerve wracking. The horses painted by the twins seemed alive with intelligent eyes and bright spirits. With a little stretch of the imagination, they could be heard to whinny.

"Were there any conditions placed on the award?" asked Buck.

"As a matter of fact," Afta said, "after completing our course of study, we must commit to working full time for a period of two years with the State of Louisiana in educating other craftsmen and craftswomen about mural painting."

"The State and federal governments have lots of buildings with loads of space crying out for murals," said Beafore.

"Walls of libraries and convention centers in the big cities of Louisiana were designed for an artist like Goya or Sargent," Beafore said, then realized her sister was motioning to add a point.

"It's like the 1930s, when FDR created the WPA as part of his New Deal," said Afta.

"WPA is the Works Project Administration," Beafore explained. "Hundreds of skilled artists were hired and paid to fill spaces inside public buildings with their talent and creativity during the Great Depression."

"Yes," Rudi said. "I remember my parents telling me how millions of people needed some income just to exist. It was a form of work relief that gave self-respect and confidence to the human spirit and impetus to the work ethic. It showcased and, you might say, even developed and increased the skills of the artisans. It lasted about eight years."

Buck then asked the twins if he could take their photo.

"Would you mind standing and putting your arms around each other's neck and pressing your cheeks next to each other?"

"You got it, Monsieur," they said in unison.

"When I count to three, please close your eyes," Buck said. "I'll change the background later to the bread section of a bakery in a Hoboken supermarket and call it 'Twins Loaf!'"

"You seem to know a lot about Germany," said Sylvia, smiling at Buck.

"As I said before, my mother was born and raised in Fischbachau, at the foot of Breitenstein, alongside the mammoth Wendelstein," Buck told them. "My father Alex was named after Alexander the Great and rose to the rank of Captain in the U.S. Marines. He was a career officer assigned to a mission in Munich by NATO, and he knew a good thing when he saw it -- namely my mother who was 21 at the time. He married her a month after meeting her in Fischbachau and literally carried her back to America after their wedding to live in the Williamsburg neighborhood of the Bronx, next door to the Mel Brooks family."

Buck blessed himself and continued. "She spoke of the grandeur of gazing at Wendelstein, next to a slightly smaller mountain called Breitenstein with Fischbachau at its doorstep. To her it was a holy place, perhaps even a shrine, picturesque beyond words or images. Forgive me, but I know that I must be repeating myself, but this is really the first time I will see it and walk through its meadows and hills just as she did."

"Why isn't your mother with you, Buck?" asked Rudi.

"Oh, she's still with me alright, right here in my heart," said Buck.

"No, I meant in person," Rudi continued.

"My mother and father were killed in the 9/11 attack in 2001 on the Twin Towers of New York," Buck answered slowly. "They were having an early breakfast inside the ground floor restaurant of the Marriott. Their remains were never found."

Buck removed a photo of them from his wallet and passed it around.

"They telephoned and left a message on our answering machine. They told me how excited they were to be in New York. Those were their last words I heard on the recording. I was just 11 years old with my father's sister, Aunt Elsie, baby-sitting when they telephoned."

"I pray that you will find your mother's birthplace, and may God protect you all the days of your life," said Sylvia.

"I hope you will find in her birthplace a dream come true, too," said Rudi.

The door of the compartment opened slowly and a middle-aged, well-dressed, bearded man wearing spectacles with lenses like the bottom of coke bottles took a seat next to Buck.

"Christ Gott," he said. "Bitte, wie lange bevor wir nach Munchen kommen?"

"He asked how much longer before we get to Munich," said Buck.

"Ah, Americans I presume," he said in slightly accented English. "Based on the smiles on your faces, I presumed you were Germans headed to the Oktoberfest."

"We are getting close to Munich central station," Buck told him, then noticed a newspaper sticking partially out of the newcomer's leather briefcase.

"Are you headed for the Oktoberfest?" Buck asked him.

"I have an appointment with a breeder to buy one of his Trakehners," the man answered. "It is an important appointment, and I must not be late."

"Well, trains in Germany run like a Swiss watch, not like a Trakehner," said Buck, who suspected that the man was Middle Eastern, based mostly on his accent and the print on his newspaper. "Your newspaper is certainly not German or English."

"Arabic," answered the man who quickly became defensive. "Are you a spy or just curious about me?" he slowly asked Buck in a suspicious manner.

"On the contrary, I am a photojournalist with a curious mind for anything related to history."

"You can put your mind to rest. I import coffee from the mountains of Haraan, Yemen. Farmers there carry on a tradition of growing and harvesting beans known for centuries as the best tasting beans in the world. A cup of coffee sells for 14 euros in Munich and around $17 U.S. in Seattle."

"And your name is …?" asked Rudi.

"My name is Khalid Najjar Khalid. Some call me irascible," he answered laughing, "but you can call me 'Cal'. I speak German because I was born in Germany. I also speak Arabic because my parents are Yemeni."

"Yumpin' Yemeni," smiled Buck, with a pronounced twang. "Just an expression I picked up from watching classic movies of the Old West. It was an expression of surprise, spoken by old cowpokes… Obviously, I'm surprised to travel with a Yemeni."

"What breed of horses did you say you were buying?" Rudi asked Cal.

"Trakehners," answered Cal, who then pushed his newspaper deeper inside his briefcase front pocket so that it was no longer visible. "The Saudi Royal Family is interested in this breed, perhaps obsessed in importing them for possible competition in the Olympics."

"Well, if you ever need someone to take professional photos of your horses," said Buck, smiling, "I'm your man, a wizard with the camera and computer graphics. Here's my card. Look me up if you're ever in America."

"Where are you staying in Germany?" asked Cal, who noticed Buck's address in New Jersey.

"I am in limbo at this moment in time," Buck answered and explained why he was on his way to Fischbachau. "Oh, by the way, if you need a painting or two of your horses, those two beautiful twins are your best choice. They are beginning a fellowship awarded by the State of Louisiana, and I am their unofficial agent!"

Cal thought for a moment, and asked, "Where did you say you were on your way to?"

"Fischbachau," repeated Buck.

Cal lifted his eyes to the ceiling because the name rang a bell in his mind. Suddenly, the compartment door slammed open and a handsome older and operatic conductor in an immaculate uniform poked his head inside. He bellowed at the top of his voice, *"Letzter Halt. München Hauptbahnhof. Raus."*

"That means 'Last stop. Munich Central Station. Get out'," said Buck. "This may be a good time to warn you again about protecting your luggage and wallet. It's Oktoberfest in Munich. Thousands will be embarking here, mostly from Germany. According to the tourist guidebook, you will recognize the national sports clubs by the dominant colors of their banners such as blue and white for Bavarians and black and white for Berliners. Women will be sporting their native dirndls with low-cut bodices, just like the dresses worn by the twins; men have tan lederhosen with red suspenders, dark boots, and green felt hats."

Buck continued with his advisory and told them that when they see the crowded Hauptbahnhof after they arrive in Munich, they will realize that there is security in forming a small group rather than winging it alone.

"There is less chance of losing your wallet to a pickpocket," he told them.

"You seem to know a lot about security, for someone who's making his first trip outside America," said Rudi.

"I talk to as many people about travel as possible," Buck answered. "I also studied major tour guides on Germany and read as many magazines and newspapers as possible about festivals because the photos are so revealing. Each tells more than a thousand words. As for pickpockets, they bring out the best and worst of society. After I return to Hoboken I'm planning to do a story with photographs -- not about the actual Oktoberfest -- but about people who are susceptible to pickpockets."

He paused and shook his head from side to side and advised them again.

"Please be on guard. Remember that pickpockets will be looking for a schmuck and will relieve him or her of their money. They wait with bated breath for a field day. Stay close to one another. Keep a tight grip on your valuables. You can expect a lot of bumping into people, especially many who may already be a little tipsy from consuming too much alcohol."

Cal shook Buck's hand and thanked Buck for his advice and told everyone he would be leaving them for now and perhaps might run into them again at the Oktoberfest.

"A rental car agency is my next stop."

Chapter 2

A few minutes later, after walking about 50 steps in a straight line into the central concourse, the group faced the giant electronic billboard. Their eyes scanned the arrival and departure times of nearly one hundred trains and buses. The travelers all raised their heads to inhale odors that emanated from food stalls constructed throughout the concourse. Odors of freshly grilled sausage, roast beef and meat loaf, rotisserie chicken, barbequed pork, and spare ribs floated over the concourse. Each member of the group seemed to lick their lips and longed to get in the queue.

However, Buck was busy snapping photos in all directions, then he persuaded everyone that this was no time to let food make them miss their bus connection.

Five minutes later the group, minus Cal, boarded a bus on the left side of Central Station. The last stop was Fischbachau, a picturesque folksy village near the base of the Breitenstein, about 45 kilometers south of Munich. The 40-minute drive from Munich to Fischbachau started on the autobahn.

They all settled into their seats at the rear of the bus, then they paused to collect their thoughts and have a quick look at their guide books. There was an excitement that radiated among the group.

About 20 minutes later Buck walked to the front of the bus to speak to the driver.

"Are we on schedule?" Buck asked him.

"A few minutes ahead of schedule because there is less traffic at this hour," the driver answered. "With Haim at the wheel, you are never late for a meal. But nature is calling, and I have to pull over and take a leak."

"Do I have time for a photograph?" asked Buck.

"Yes, but make it snappy which makes me happy."

"I'll snap it before you zip up the zipper on your trousers."

Buck followed about 20 paces behind the driver who disappeared into a wooded area that bordered a lake. Buck raised his camera and stared through the lens beginning at his far left then panning slowly to his right. He said out loud, "Nothing … nothing … nothing … Oh, got it… Got it… Got it!" Buck took a closer look at the first photo and exclaimed, "Ah ssshhhhiiiitttttt!"

"What has occurred?" asked Haim with alarm and in a loud voice.

"Just as I took the first photo, an owl dropped his shit in front of my lens."

"That's not possible."

"Must I show you the evidence before you will believe me?"

"No time for it now. Every second is important; get your ass back in the bus. The mountains and lake won't go away, so you can take more photos another time."

Once the driver had his bus back on the road, he explained to Buck standing nearby that an owl doesn't shit. It regurgitates and drops pellets.

"Sounds like shit to me," laughed Buck. "and it sure looked like shit!"

Buck returned to the back of the bus and rejoined his friends there. He was eager to view the photos taken at the lake. After looking them over, he walked to the front of the bus again and told the driver that he got a good photo after all.

Haim quickly glanced at Buck and asked, "Did you just tell me that you got a good photo?"

Buck said, "Yes, the second two were very good. One had the mountains on the horizon, the morning sun reflected off the waters of the lake, and a cluster of Tannenbaum trees on the left. The next one was a better one with the mountains, the morning sun, the waters of the lake, and Tannenbaum trees -- and you on the right side, pissing in an arc about six feet into something that resembles a small rainbow at its base."

Haim said to Buck, "Yes, this scene reminds me of Hoher Göll and Hintersee about 11 kilometers west of Berchtesgaden on the border between Bavaria and Austria."

Buck laughed and admitted, "I guess my professors at Lehigh were right when they said if I were to take a good photograph, it would be a miracle!"

Der Hintersee mit dem Hoher Göll
The Hintersee with the Hoher Göll
Josef Thoma

It was around 10 in the morning when Haim pulled his bus into an inlet on the right side of a two-lane country road and told everyone, "This is Fischbachau, the end of the line and right on time. With Haim at the wheel, you are never late for a meal. Thank you for traveling with Haim transit and tempus fugit."

Haim obviously was a legend in his own mind. His verses were short and cute, just like him. They all picked up their luggage and marched single file up a short hill along one side of the grand two-story Inn and past a large sign that seemed to sway from a light wind. The word "Winkelstüberl" was spelled out in colorful letters and surrounded by a garland of flowers, carved and hand-painted by a skilled folk artist.

On top of the sign was perched an Alpine crow with his yellow bill, red legs, and glossy jet-black plumage. He opened his yellow bill and gave a distinctive, shrill shriek. Buck explained that this was the bird's way of welcoming tourists with the hope that they will leave a few morsels of food later to supplement the bird's natural diet.

Once inside the Inn, two porters -- a wiry husband and considerably more muscular wife -- carried the ladies' luggage directly to their assigned rooms on the second floor.

When the group reassembled downstairs, Buck suggested a light lunch on the patio before embarking on a trek to the mountain top.

"I heard their Weisswurst sausages are to die," he exclaimed. "They're very delicious with all the herbs blended in by the butcher. Tell the waitress you want them with a half-liter of beer, some mustard, and two pretzels -- and leave it at that."

Everyone then gathered quickly in a nice shaded area. Red plastic tables and chairs rested on finely crushed gravel. They gazed at the mountain peak of Wendelstein on the left and the waiter told them it was about 6,000 feet up in a gradual climb. He then told them that on the right was Breitenstein with Fischbachau nestled at its foot. The path for climbers ended at 5,300 feet.

They wondered if they could climb Breitenstein in an afternoon. Then Sylvia felt inspired and started to sing softly the lyrics from *The*

Sound of Music. Birds were heard to twitter in harmony as geraniums swayed in their flower boxes attached to the ledges of the windows on the front side of the Inn. It was a magical moment for those who appreciated and recognized such times.

After lunch, Buck surprised them by apologizing for bowing out of the climb because of his vertigo.

"Forgive me for passing up this climb but I get dizzy from climbing a six-foot ladder, and I have this fear of heights. You wouldn't want me to tumble down the mountainside, would you?"

The climbers wished Buck good fortune and headed toward the dirt road leading to Breitenstein. Rudi pressed the start button on his stopwatch to enter the time of departure so he would know the point of no return.

Buck elected to rent a bicycle from the concession next to the Inn. The elderly owner, Tutz Suite, told him, "Keep an eye out for bears. By all means, remember not to invade their territory and they won't invade yours. If you want insurance, it's $10 U.S. a day."

"That seems cheap," said Buck.

"Well, I could charge you more for flats and damage if you want me to," said Tutz, jesting.

"Oh, I thought you were talking about insurance for bears," Buck said.

"Bears don't need insurance, my friend," Tutz answered. "Just bear in mind that this is their homeland, not yours to invade."

Buck thanked him and began to pedal his bike along the two-lane road beside the Inn in search of a forest with a meadow-like shrine his mother spoke of so often while Buck was growing up in Hoboken.

Two hours later Buck was pedaling toward Fischbachau on a one-lane country road that seemed to divide a forest. He was strengthened by the smell of pine trees, probably Tannenbaums, and the pronounced odor of ozone. About a half-mile later he felt the grind of his front wheel on the road and realized his bike had a flat tire. He turned his bike upside down onto the roadway's left shoulder to draw attention to his predicament, then he walked (unknowingly) through a bush of poison ivy to lean against the trunk of a tree nearby.

The sound of a motor made Buck look to his right. It was a pickup truck that rose slowly on the horizon. A crazy thought crossed his mind: the truck moved like a giant spider creeping out of nowhere.

The driver drifted to a slow halt without braking too much. He was driving a beat-up and rusty pickup truck, a German-made Ford with at least 15 years of wear and tear. The driver appeared to be a muscular, rugged-looking man, about 45 to 50 years of age. His most distinguishing features were his green, battered-felt Alpine hat pulled down to his eyebrows, his piercing eyes, and overgrown moustache -- twice the size of Groucho Marx's.

Unbeknownst to the driver, Buck snapped a picture of him with his camera, a profile of the driver looking straight ahead. However, as the driver slowed his truck as he passed Buck, he noticed through the driver's side mirror that Buck held his camera close to his chest with one hand.

Buck walked a few steps toward him, introduced himself, and asked for a lift back to the Inn.

"I assume you are a good Samaritan and willing to help me with a flat tire, otherwise why would you stop?"

The man recognized something peculiar about Buck's accent.

"You're an American out in the middle of the woods with a camera?" he asked Buck slowly and forcefully. "Are you spying on me?"

"Spying?" Buck asked. "Far from it. I am a freelance photo-journalist …from Hoboken."

"Where the f_ck is Hoboken?" the man asked with growing anxiety and impatience.

"On the northern border of *New Joysee*, along the Hudson River," Buck answered, pronouncing his home state like a reality TV star.

"Are you a Christian?"

"Yes, I am a Christian."

"And your mother and father?"

"My mother was born and raised in this area. She was Jewish."

"And your father?"

"He was born in America and was a career officer, a Captain, in the U.S. Marines."

"I didn't ask for his occupation, did I?"

"I don't know what you're after but forget about asking any more questions about my family. It's really none of your business."

"So, you are a half breed… *half and half,* so to speak."

"Are you going to give me a lift or are you just jerking me around?" asked Buck, growing impatient. "I thought you were a good Samaritan."

The man told him to put his bike into the bed of his truck and to take his place in the passenger seat beside him. He then proceeded to drive for about five minutes and turned into the right side of a fork in a one-lane country road. He then slammed on his brakes so abruptly that Buck hit his head on the dashboard. He was dazed for a minute or two until the driver pulled him out of the passenger's seat and stood him upright with his back against the front right fender.

"Take your clothes off," the man shouted like a drill sergeant giving orders to a troop of trainees.

"Pardon me," Buck answered. "What did you say?"

"I don't like repeating myself. Must I repeat myself?"

"What's going on here?"

Buck studied the man's face. It was wrinkled and mottled with a slight icy tinge. Buck took a closer look again at his piercing eyes and lips turned down with a pointed chin. "This is one cat you don't want to mess with," he said to himself.

The driver removed a pistol from inside his waist belt and pressed it under Buck's chin. "Remove all your clothes. Your clothes or your life."

Buck was confused but realized he was dealing with a man who was deranged, perhaps even paranoid.

"Is this a strip search? Can't we talk this thing out? You keep the bike and take off, please, and no questions asked and no regrets."

"You can't change my mind," said the driver. "My mind is made up. You Jew dog!"

"This is absurd…crazy…insane. You've got my bike, my wallet, my money, my passport, my cell phone, my airline and train tickets. Isn't that enough?" asked Buck, stuttering to get his words out. "Are you going to kill me? If so, do it now."

"I'll repeat myself just once," the driver told Buck. "Let me make this perfectly clear. Your clothes or your life!"

"Whatever you say, sir. If you want my clothes, they're yours."

"Throw your hat, sunglasses, and shoes in, too."

"You are thorough, man, I mean sir. But forget any notion of surrendering my Stetson and Porsche Sport sunglasses. You'll have to kill me first. I never take them off -- not for no one and not at no time."

The driver ignored Buck's response as meaningless and quickly gathered his clothes including his camera and rolled them into a bundle. He then asked Buck to put his bike over them so they wouldn't blow out when he resumed driving.

Except for his Stetson, Porsche Sport sunglasses, and wristwatch, Buck was left as naked as a newborn baby in the middle of the forest. He watched the rusty truck move slowly down the road and felt enraged.

"This must be a nightmare. This cannot be happening to me," he murmured out loud.

He slapped his face several times with increasing force, then he lifted his head as far back as it would stretch and howled like a wolf. His cry pierced the sky and echoed off the trees. Now he began to fear for his survival and wondered how he would survive if he came face to face with a bear.

"Up popped the Devil, but this Devil is a monster, a real person, more menacing, more threatening," Buck said to himself. "But this is not the time to feel sorry for myself."

Buck looked repeatedly at his watch with watery eyes and noted the time. "That robbery by the road bandit took less than three minutes," he said to himself. "These three minutes will not be engraved on my tombstone."

He raised his sunglasses enough to cup his hands and fingers as if holding a pair of binoculars and watched the pick-up truck disappear up and over a knoll. Buck was consumed with anger and fortified by revenge building up in his psyche. He raised his fists in anger one last time and shook them in the direction of the truck.

"You put a gun to my head, you bastard. If it's the last thing I do on this earth, I swear, so help me God, I will hunt you down like a bear."

Buck began to talk to himself out loud as he walked along the dirt road. "Logic says that I should follow the direction of his truck and see where it leads to. God, I have a question for you. Why would a man want to rob me of my clothes? Was he after my Ralph Lauren jacket or Wrangler western jeans? Could he be a clotheshorse with a serious vitamin deficiency?"

Unable to get a response, Buck tried to reconcile everything that had happened. He said a prayer. "Please, God, help me to find a way out of my misery. You have never deserted me in my hour of need. Give me now the strength and wisdom to survive."

Without warning, Buck heard God tell him, "Lighten up, *kid*. This is not the end of the world."

"That's okay for you to say, but you didn't have a gun under your chin, did you...and is *kid* the right word for you to use to describe me?"

God never answered him.

The thought of finding something in the forest to hide his groin entered his mind but quickly faded when he saw that both sides of the road were lined with poison ivy.

"Oh, shit," Buck said to himself. "I remember my freshman year in college when my fraternity brothers dropped me in a field of corn lined with poison ivy bushes as part of the initiation. Two days later they visited me in the hospital when I made it abundantly clear that I had scratched any previous interest I had in joining their fraternity."

Buck soon realized that he was a tenderfoot at heart. He walked as lightly as possible on the part-dirt and part-gravel road, but each footstep was like walking on pins and needles.

This moment in time brought back memories of the days when he was about eight years old and dressed as an Indian brave and played cowboys and Indians with friends in the backyard of his Hoboken home. He now remembered every pebble and stone he stepped on while wearing moccasins.

One hour passed quickly as Buck estimated that he had covered about three miles. Then he noticed a road to the right. It was solid dirt without gravel and clearly showed tire tracks. He followed it for another quarter mile until a heavenly picturesque green and gold meadow appeared. It was filled with sunflowers in full bloom in front of rows of hops.

Suddenly, a light drizzle of rain with just the right coolness began to fall. The raindrops covered every part of his body. The steady rainfall seemed to lower his temperature to a point where he began to feel the worst events of the day had disappeared from his psyche. He smiled, inhaled the freshness of the drizzle, and wiped his hands over his body as if drying himself after a shower.

Buck checked his watch and it was close to 5 p.m. In the distant outer reaches of the meadow he noticed horses grazing on the slopes of hills. He thought of the lost opportunity to take a photograph or two that National Geographic would be eager to pay for. Then a rainbow suddenly emerged with one end behind a two-story farmhouse on the left side of the meadow. Smoke was rising from its chimney, which meant someone might be inside to provide help.

Buck knocked hard on the front door, pressed his ear against it for five seconds, then pounded with his fist. He heard the sound of a deadbolt that slammed across the back of the door. Seconds later, when the door was fully opened, the back light from inside the house made it so the two figures appeared like silhouettes. Buck guessed that they were probably a mother and daughter.

When they caught sight of Buck standing on the doorstep with his hands covering his groin, their eyes widened. Buck unexpectedly sneezed and cupped his mouth with his hands, exposing his groin.

The mother, slightly shorter and heavier, put her hands to the sides of her mouth and said, "Oh. Gesundheit!"

The daughter, taller and well proportioned, smiled broadly and roared like a lion, "Whoa…Oh…Wow!"

An instant later, a large golden retriever burst between them and jumped onto Buck with a force that knocked him backward to the ground. The dog covered Buck's body and began licking his neck, ears, and cheeks in that order. It whimpered excitedly at the prospect of finding a new friend.

"I think he likes me, Ma'am," Buck told the heavier one.

"My name is not Ma'am, it's Marlene; and 'he' is a 'she' -- a girl dog," she answered. "Schatze, for Christ's sake, get off and leave him be."

"Here, girl!" said the daughter, "and my name is Erika."

"No, don't call her off yet," said Buck, pleading nervously. "Please give me something like a robe to cover my body?"

"Wait right there," said Marlene.

"Don't move a muscle," said Erika. "That goes for you too, Schatze."

Marlene returned quickly with a friar's frock and handed it to Buck. She told him, "It was left here about a year ago by one of the monks from the Kloster Maxlrain nearby. That is a famous monastery and brewery."

"There's another one close by, too, a Benedictine order, I believe," said Erika who watched Buck as he turned away from the door and donned the frock in a flash.

"For heaven's sake, Erika, give him some privacy, please," said Marlene. "When you're able to stand on two feet again, you are welcome to come inside."

Minutes later they were seated comfortably at the dinner table inside a large farm house that dated from the late 19th century. Buck's roving eyes then caught sight of a large cuckoo clock that hung on a far wall. Its mechanical insides gave off a loud ticking sound. Its face was very attractive and contained a green door over a white enamel dial surrounded by hand-carved wooden images of birds and leaves.

The grand room was cozy and reminiscent of a 19th century rustic interior. Its warmth was enhanced by the stone fireplace and antique stove.

"Gemütlich," said Erika. "That means cozy in German."

"Welcome to Villa Allesin," said Marlene. "That's the name my husband gave this farmhouse and its 50 acres of sunflowers and hops, forest, and hills."

Erika said, " 'Alle' in German is 'All' in English, and 'Sunde' in German is 'Sin' in English. But my father gave it a half-German half-English spelling and pronunciation. Don't ask me why he did that."

Marlene explained that this grand room was the old part of the house, constructed in 1880. She also mentioned that her husband had inherited the property from his parents who bought it from a Jewish farmer whose daughter married an American soldier.

That comment struck a chord with Buck, who was unable to assimilate it fully because of other things flashing through his mind.

Erika then acknowledged that a modern addition of three bedrooms and two baths were added a year after her mother married.

"I have to confess that my husband was the epitome of a misanthrope," said Marlene. "It began many years ago when his father was negotiating to buy this house from a Jewish family. They kept increasing their price for the property that included some of the richest land in the valley. Max -- my husband --ignored that fact that his parents were indecisive and failed to make up their mind when a lower offer was on the table. He made a mistake in thinking the price for the property would go down, but instead it went up each year and substantially, too. He never understood the right to bargain until after he became a veterinarian and bred and sold horses."

"Perhaps it is time to tell you something of myself," Buck said and went on to describe his birthplace in Hoboken, New Jersey. He admitted that his mother said that she went into labor in Hoboken only because she didn't want her baby born on the train that had just stopped at Lackawanna Terminal, the previous station.

"How would you like that name for your birthplace associated with the thousands of forms you fill out during a lifetime?" Buck asked and chuckled. "My father was a career officer in the U.S. Marines and planted an interest in history in me. Whenever he could, he would take me around to historic places -- monuments, battlefields, and museums and introduce me to people who told the most fascinating stories. These experiences had an impact on my consciousness when I was a child that continues to this day."

"Did you attend and graduate from college?" asked Marlene.

"I graduated from Lehigh," answered Buck.

"What is Lehigh?" asked Erika, "and where is Lehigh?"

"Lehigh is Lehigh University in Bethlehem, Pennsylvania; not Bethlehem in Israel."

"And what did you major in?" Erika asked.

"Girls, big and small, fat and thin. I never met a girl I didn't like," Buck answered. "Actually, I majored in photography and minored in history. Girls came running when they saw me with a Canon around my neck."

Marlene and Erika looked at each other and smiled.

"I bet you had to fight them off," said Erika.

"All except one," Buck answered. "She wanted to marry a millionaire. She had her sights set on a millionaire."

"And what did you want, Buck?" asked Marlene.

"I wanted a friend who believed that I *can* be better than myself and *will* be better than myself," said Buck.

"I don't believe you would be happy with someone who wanted a millionaire even if you were a millionaire," added Marlene.

"And what do you have your sights set on now?" asked Erika.

"The birthplace of my mother," answered Buck. "I want to feel her vibrations again if I can find the home that she grew up in, that area and environment, and perhaps meet some of her friends and relatives who knew her."

"Well, you don't know us from women on the moon, so to speak," said Marlene, "but we would be willing to help you in any way that is legal and not an invasion of someone's privacy."

"Ever since she passed away," said Buck, "I have had dreams of finding out more about her and her early life."

"It seems that you have unleashed your imagination about her growing up in Bavaria. Perhaps later you can tell us your vision so we can get a better idea how to steer you in the right direction," said Marlene.

"Is it true that a photograph is worth a thousand words?" asked Erika.

"Yes, I believe it is true," answered Buck, "but those words are not chiseled in marble and are different for each person looking at the photo. One of my idols is the film director George Stevens who covered the final months of World War II in Germany and was deeply affected after inspecting the horrible conditions of Nazi concentration camps. From that point on in his life he was intent on making films about people who faced a daily crisis, films that would dig into your soul and forcefully pull your heart strings. A good example was the film *The Diary of Anne Frank*."

Marlene asked, "When you were young, were you as curious and imaginative with a camera as you were curious and imaginative by nature?"

"Yes," Buck responded with a chuckle. "Even before I had a camera, when I saw something I wanted to remember I framed it with my hands as though I were taking a photo."

"When you were in college, were you recognized and appreciated as a future photojournalist by your professors?" asked Erika.

"Depends on your point of view, I guess," answered Buck. "The camera was an extension of my consciousness. On campus I was known as the Miracle Photographer. My professors said that if my photograph was good, it was a miracle!"

"Well, my mother's soup is no miracle, but close to it. Of course, I am a little biased, but I believe in miracles. It's a miracle that you made it to our doorstep. So, please begin to taste the best and freshest homemade chicken soup in the world," Erika said with gusto. "My mother is famous for her soup in these parts, so everyone says."

"Please don't misunderstand me," said Buck, "but my appetite for food has been destroyed by an arrogant road bandit who put a gun to my head and threatened to kill me. His conduct was downright criminal to say the least."

"You're kidding, aren't you?" asked Marlene.

Buck explained everything in detail from the time he rented his bike to his arrival on their doorstep. He described everything in a series of quick flashbacks. He even admitted to taking a photo of the road bandit.

"I would show you what he looked like," Buck said. "But he stole my camera along with everything else."

Marlene said, "I find it hard to believe someone in Fischbachau would commit such a horrible act. On the contrary, most people around here are so friendly, except perhaps for my husband."

While they began to stir their still too-hot soup, Buck asked them, "Did you know that when a monk removes his frock, his religious powers and his sanctity are removed along with it?"

He paused to taste his soup. "Pardon me, but everything is a little crazy today. Let me apologize for asking such a bizarre question. I can't help wondering if the monk's powers will pass on to me. I can use all the support from anyone able to help me, especially from God."

Marlene and Erika nodded and smiled as they were beginning to understand and accept their new guest from America.

"Your soup tastes fabulous, just like the chicken vegetable soup my mother made," Buck told them. "I hope I can find out more about her while I'm here because she was born in this area. No one had a better mother and father than me. My father was so happy when he described how he met my mother that he actually cried. While growing up, I realized that when he cried was when he was happiest."

"You were blessed, Buck," said Erika.

"I must tell you that I was just 11 when they were taken away from me and killed in the 9/11 ISIS attack on the Twin Towers."

Marlene and Erika both reached across and placed their hands over his.

"I get a telepathic signal from you about kindness," said Marlene. "Mental telepathy, I presume."

"Perhaps some of the monk's powers from his cloak have passed on to me," said Buck. "I always believe that kindness was one of the most important character traits a human can manifest. Take this chicken soup for example. Each vegetable is selected and added to increase the flavor and nutrition, just like each act of kindness may be added for the joy and welfare of another person. It is given freely and without any expectation of a return in equal proportion. And it wouldn't hurt to toss in a little bit of tolerance."

"That is beautifully expressed," Erika answered, squeezing his hand.

"Do you live here alone with just your daughter and husband?" Buck asked Marlene with growing curiosity. "I mean, are workers or farmhands around too?"

"We have some help to grow and harvest sunflowers and hops. But we both help my husband if you want to call him that. He's a veterinarian who specializes in breeding Trakehners and can do the work of three men, believe me," said Marlene, appearing five years younger than her age of 45. "He works from sunup to sundown."

"He comes and goes as he pleases" said Erika, looking very mature at 21. "He's like the wind. He has his own timetable and work schedule. Behind his back, we often refer to him as '*Mad Max*'."

"From my studies of psychology at the university," said Buck, "I learned that people live in several worlds and each is constantly evolving. Max seems presently to be in a disgraceful world of his own making."

"In reality, he's quick tempered and lately has grown into a bit of a tyrant," Marlene exclaimed. "He treats us worse than servants. He is more like a commandant of a concentration camp. His conduct is bizarre most of the time, and he seems to be increasingly ill-tempered and combative lately. He trusts no one and is constantly looking over his shoulder because he believes people are spying on him."

"He often sleeps in his hut on the mountainside…to be closer to his horses and his laboratory," said Erika.

"At the end of my second year of law school," said Marlene, "I was engaged to a classmate for two months."

"I didn't know that, Mom," said Erika.

"I don't think he did, either," laughed Marlene. "At least he didn't act as though we were engaged – ever after he gave me the ring! A year later I met Max and was swept away by his charm and will power. I was 23 and had just graduated from law school in Munich when we were married. In the beginning he was friendly, affectionate, tender, and a good companion. But two or three years after Erika was born everything gradually changed from better to worse. Now he can be threatening, but so far he hasn't hurt us physically. However, for the past four years he has grown into a living monster; at nighttime, a dreaded nightmare."

"I dread, too, every moment I have to live with my father, if you want to call him that," said Erika. "I wanted to study the piano but he refused to let me. We, my mother and I, conspired for me to study privately after class. I love music in all forms."

Buck let out a deep breath and said, "It appears that Max is a disciple of the devil…I assume that he at least puts food on the table and is the breadwinner of the family."

"We have no financial problems, knock on wood," said Marlene.

Marlene struggled to explain her predicament. "I'm not good at being humble and have no explanation of why I would stay married to a man I had fallen out of love with. It is something I cannot express in words. Call it fear of striking out on my own…fear for me and my daughter…fear of retaliation and retribution from Max."

Buck put his hand on Marlene's, squeezed it gently, and told her that Max will be punished inevitably, but not by God. He looked a long time at his bowl of soup and decided to eat some more of it, then rose from the table to study the photos on the mantle over the fireplace.

"I see photos of both you and Erika here and can see why your husband married you, Marlene. You were -- and still are --gorgeous. But I don't see any photos of your husband."

"He burned them, all of them. During the past four years, he became delirious and combative if anyone ever took a photo of him," said Erika.

"I am beginning to get a picture of him in my mind and it's not a pretty picture," said Buck. "What is the breed of the horses he bred?"

"Trakehners," Erika told him. "My father is an expert in cross-breeding them with Arabian bloodlines and raising them until they are sold, lately to Saudi Arabia royal families. He is famous around these parts for his breeding knowhow."

"This is the second time I have heard this word recently. Exactly what is a Trakehner?" Buck asked.

Marlene glowed when she told him, "Their rectangular build is unique. They have a long sloping shoulder, good hindquarters, short cannon bones, and a medium-to-long crested and well-set neck. Their head is finely chiseled in a classic way dating back centuries. It's narrow at the muzzle with a broad forehead. Furthermore, the Trakehner is known for its impulsion and suspension, which gives it its floating trot."

"Oh, it sounds like a dream to ride," Buck enthused. "I would love to ride one."

"You ride?" Erika asked, wide-eyed.

"Yes, I competed in Western riding events, and I've worked around barns a lot." Buck swallowed his stein of beer and burped.

"Our beer is as fresh as a newborn foal," said Erika, "because we get it delivered like a pizza, but in a barrel directly from the brewery at Kloster Maxlrain."

Erika tried to refill his stein but Buck covered it with his hand just as she started pouring. He licked his hand and told her, "Waste not, want not."

Erika continued the conversation by telling him, "Trakehners' best feature for riders is that they are trainable and athletic even when they are a bit headstrong. Trakehners have won gold and silver medals in dressage in the Olympics too."

"Max began to cross breed Arabian blood into the Trakehner about five years ago," Marlene admitted. "Here is a bronze by the great French animalier sculptor Francois Barye. This isn't a Trakehner-Arabian cross, but it is very close to Max's ideal horse."

She handed him a 10-inch high bronze sculpture by Barye for him to study closely.

Cheval Demi-Sang (Tête Levée)
Half-Blood Horse with Head Raised
Antoine Louis Barye

"This is the first time I ever held one of his bronzes in my own hands," answered Buck. "I've seen an array of his works at the Walters Art Gallery in Baltimore many years ago but wasn't allowed to touch or even photograph one."

"Max should be back any time now," said Marlene. "I heard him pull into the garage about an hour or two ago. He seemed agitated and told me that he was going into the forest to pick some mushrooms for our evening meal. But he may have changed his mind and gone to his office and lab, which are inside a salt mine at the far end of the meadow."

Marlene then took a closer look at Buck's face and arms. There were red blotches everywhere that Buck unconsciously continued to scratch. She surmised that he had a case of poison ivy and questioned him about it.

"I had my clothes on when the bike had a flat tire. Afterward, I walked through a bush of that stuff. It probably covered my pants then soon found its way to my face and arms," said Buck.

"After what you have been through, I hope you will spend the night with us," said Erika. "You can stay in the guest room if you like."

"If that's an invitation," said Buck gratefully, "I accept."

Marlene placed a bottle of schnapps and three shot glasses on the table. "I know from experience that a shot before bedtime makes one sleepy."

"It's probably a fairy tale but a shot is known to work wonders when your mind wanders and you get the itch to wander, too," said Erika.

"Good for poison ivy?" asked Buck. "I may have wandered inadvertently into a patch or two."

"That and that other itch, too," Erika said, "the itch for revenge."

The cuckoo clock on the far wall started to strike the hour. However, when the door opened and the bird emerged, the cuckoo could only pronounce the first syllable, "Coo," which was repeated five times.

Buck belched and followed that up with a giant yawn as he started to nod off.

Marlene recognized that Buck was tired and it was time to show him to his room upstairs. She escorted him to the stairway, followed by Erika a few steps behind.

"It's time for bed, but I doubt if you will sleep deeply after such a horrendous experience with the wicked road bandit of the South," said Marlene sympathetically as she wrapped her arm around his.

They took a few steps up the stairs, then Buck turned when Erika called out in a loud voice, "Buck, if there is anything you need during the night, all you have to do is call me. All you have to do is…"

"Whistle?" asked Buck with a devilish smile.

"No," answered Erika. "This is not Martinique. This is Bavaria. All you have to do is yodel. You know how to yodel, don't you, Buck? You just put your lips together and blow!"

Marlene tightened her grip on Buck's arm, continued to lead him up the stairway, and told him, "I think my daughter has seen too many Humphrey Bogart and Lauren Bacall films, or at least she has seen *To Have and Have Not* too often!"

"I like her imagination and, more important, I like her sense of humor," Buck answered. "It disarms tension and anxiety. It's a nice thought to keep in mind, especially tonight."

Once Buck settled into his bed and drew down his covers, the bedtime hours passed slowly. He tossed and turned throughout the night from the recurring nightmares of his ordeal. He asked God why this was happening to him but received no answer. His whole life passed through his mind laboriously.

High anxiety made him quiver as he rolled from side to side in his bed. Luckily for others in the house, his moans and groans and creaking sounds of the wood frame of his bed stayed inside the walls of his room.

However, a more distressing ailment continued to bother him.

He unconsciously had scratched himself all over his body and spread the poison ivy from head to foot.

"What is worse, the nightmares or the itch?" he asked himself while lifting his head off the pillow and wiping the sweat from his face. He then noticed a stream of moonlight that fell through a window behind his headboard and bounced off the wooden floor onto an old slant-top desk. A strange glow mysteriously floated around it. He remembered his mother buying one for his room in New Jersey and telling him that it was a reproduction of an antique one very much like the one she had in her home in Germany. Seeing that bureau not only brought back memories of his mother but seemed to lower the need to scratch the itch and paved a way for him to drift into a twilight sleep.

CHAPTER 3

The morning sun filtered through a window on the opposite side of Buck's bed. Moments later, Buck heard a rooster crow and smelled the aroma of freshly made coffee. It brought a smile to his face. It was the biggest smile he had smiled in a long time. He remembered how his mother was delighted to serve German-style coffee bought from an importer in Hoboken. He yawned repeatedly and struggled to fully open his eyes until they were splashed with cold water. When he looked into a mirror he saw that his face and arms were covered with red blotches.

At the breakfast table Buck asked Marlene and Erika if Max had returned home.

"No sign or word or holler, as far as I know," said Erika. "But Buck, I am afraid I have some bad news for you. It's called poison ivy, and you are covered with it from head to toes."

"The itching has lessened a little," he told them.

"We have Calamine lotion that might dry up your rash and soothe the itch," said Erika. "We also have medicine to drink that helps eradicate poison ivy from inside your body."

Fifteen minutes later Buck suggested that it was about time to have a look around the property for Max. "Nothing ventured, nothing gained," he told Marlene and Erika.

Once outside Buck passed the garage with its doors wide open. He recognized immediately that the beat-up truck inside was the one the road bandit used when robbing him. In the bed of the truck were his clothes, shoes, camera, and bike.

"Hold it right here," Buck exclaimed. "These *are* my clothes… camera…bike…wallet and iPhone."

Twenty minutes later Buck was wearing his own clothes again as everyone headed across the field of sunflowers to look for Max. Before leaving, Buck was apprehensive and asked for a rifle to protect himself.

As Marlene handed Buck a rifle, he asked, "Why did you marry him and not complete your degree? Please pardon me for probing here."

"Max was strong, physically and mentally…and sure of himself. What did I know about love at 23? I heard love makes the world go 'round, but planet earth must have slipped on its axis for me."

Everyone just shook their heads in puzzlement as Buck assured them that he did not blame them for Max's actions and was grateful for their hospitality and concern for his welfare.

After crossing the meadow and entering the fringe of the forest, Marlene said, "Let's not rush it here. We really don't have a clue what to expect. Don't make a sound."

"Don't even break a twig," said Erika nervously.

Everything strangely became eerie and the only sound heard was the chirping of crickets.

"Only male crickets chirp," said Buck. "On their wings they have a file and scraper attached."

"Do you mean like a file and scraper found in a forge or foundry?" asked Erika.

"Yes, but crickets have different ways of creating their individual chirping sounds," said Buck. "Male crickets are trying to attract females."

Buck turned to Erika. "Wish I could chirp to attract your attention."

"No need for you to chirp," said Erika, who then slapped Buck on his back. "You already have my complete attention."

A few minutes later Marlene led everyone through the forest and into a clearing about 50 feet in diameter. She pointed toward an old oak tree and told Buck that here was an area in the forest where mushrooms grew.

All three then slowly spread out in slightly different directions.

Moments later, Marlene let out a scream that sent shivers up everyone's spine.

"Over here," she said horrified.

She recognized the face and body of her husband. The blood covering his face and head still seemed to be a little moist. She hugged her daughter and told her that it may be too gruesome for her to see. "*Schade,*" exclaimed Marlene, using the German word for "what a pity."

Buck looked down at a 10-foot long tree that had fallen near a giant oak tree. Its trunk was partially rotted, probably from a lightning strike years ago. About 10 feet behind it was the body of a large man with his right hand gripping his Alpine hat. His head was clamped tightly by the steel pointers of a large bear trap. His skull had been crushed by the impact. His eyes and mouth were wide open. The top set of his teeth was frozen to the right of his mouth while the lower set had shifted to the far left side. Buck surmised that the dead man had been in the act of grinding his teeth. It was a scene out of a horror movie.

Buck, Marlene, and Erika walked slowly in a ring around the body, studying it carefully. Buck noticed that the man's legs were not tangled and his shoes left a track on the ground, indicating he probably backed up and fell over the tree trunk.

"It looks as if he was moving backwards and struggled to get his feet under him," said Buck. "Have a close look at the indentation where the heels of his work shoes are dug into the earth."

"That's the first time I ever saw Max with his hat off," said Marlene.

"You mean to say he slept with it on, too?" asked Buck.

"That's not all he did with his hat on," Marlene said apologetically.

Erika noticed a banana peel stuck to the bottom of Max's right shoe. "Although it may seem disingenuous and facetious," she said, "I suspect he slipped on a banana peel!"

"A little levity is always a relief but this is not the time for it," said her mother.

"Now we have a 'who done it,' don't we?" asked Buck. "Frankly, I am relieved. This may be the end of my vow for vengeance and revenge."

Marlene, with her usual calm nature, told Buck, "I remember something about Shakespeare that I learned from my literature class at the University. I will paraphrase it but in essence, one does not escape punishment for carrying out his evil revenge. Over the years I could have sought revenge against Max for his mistreatment of us, but I managed to keep my feelings and inclinations under control."

"You're right as rain," answered Buck.

"I made a concerted effort to abide by the law and try to become a lawyer who would not seek revenge from unexpected sources," Marlene continued. "People are capable of acting worse than animals, but we must learn to control our forces otherwise we are no better than animals. In other words, there is no room for *tit-for-tat*."

"Good advice," said Buck, "but although I may not seek revenge, let it be known to one and all that I will never forgive."

"This is one case where we can't blame the butler," said Erika. "In most killings, it is assumed first off that the butler did it!"

"If Max were chased by a bear and fell or stumbled backward into the trap, wouldn't the bear tear him to pieces?" asked Erika. "After all, he was trapped in his own trap and no way out."

"Not necessarily," answered her mother. "If the bear smelled blood, he might do just that...tear him apart. Are there any tracks from a bear around the body?"

"What does a bear track look like?" asked Buck.

Marlene showed Buck images of bear tracks that had been

downloaded to her cell phone. She pointed out that the inner toe is the smallest, the opposite of human feet, and there is an additional pad called the carpal pad that often is not visible.

"Looks like a baseball glove to me," answered Buck, laughing. "It will be impossible to find a clear print with all this debris from the forest scattered everywhere."

"Yes," said Erika, "this can be quite unbearable!"

For the next 15 minutes they scoured the area for foot prints, but none were found. Marlene admitted that the death scene may have been violated by everyone's inadvertently walking around and leaving their own footprints, but there was nothing anyone could do about that now.

Buck took more than 50 photos to document the death scene, and perhaps to show investigators later. Buck had always thought that taking a photograph was recording a moment in time and having it for posterity. He felt that if you failed to do that the moment in time never existed.

As Buck inhaled the ozone generated by the forest and let his breath out slowly he began to gain a feeling of relief as though a huge burden had been lifted from his shoulders.

"A great American, Will Rogers, once said, 'I never met a man I didn't like.' I wonder how Max will answer God if he ever reaches the pearly gates of Heaven and is asked, 'Did you ever meet a man you liked?'"

"There may be an opportunity for some good to come from your years of suffering," Buck said thoughtfully to Marlene and Erika. "I can see doing a photo journalism piece about Mad Max with all the proceeds going to you and Erika."

"Absolutely not," Marlene said. "Now is not the time for publicity and interviews that would delve into our privacy. No invasion of privacy for now, please."

"Just because we object to your idea to do a story on Max now," said Erika, "doesn't mean we object to having you stay longer with us. Your presence can help to heal our misery, grief, and chaos."

"That's right, Erika," said Marlene. "It would be nice to get to know you better too. It's even nicer to have a real man around, someone trustworthy. When everything has been investigated and settled, I would like to revisit the idea of your doing a piece about it."

Buck paused. "Actually, for me, there is no amount of money anyone could give me to compensate for the humiliation I suffered. I think there's a story here, but perhaps you are right that this is not the time for it. It's a story of a trapper being trapped in his own trap."

Buck bowed his head and shook it from side to side. "Insensitive I am not. Ambitious and impulsive I am."

"Leave the body exactly where it is, and I'll call the police," Marlene said, motioning Buck for his cell phone. "Leave everything as it is right now, please."

"Good idea," said Buck, "and I'll take a few more photos before sundown."

Buck offered to cover Max's head with his jacket but Erika said, "Leave him *au naturel* as the French would say."

"Hey, do you get the feeling that this place is a little eerie… spooky?" asked Buck.

"Do you see or sense something we don't?" Marlene asked.

"When I look through the lens of my camera and scan the trees around us, they seem to come to life and become animated like in a fantasy film," Buck answered. "Stand beside me, one on each side of me, and hold up your arms and touch each other's fingers. Now imagine you are in the center of a circle. Half of the circle is in front of you, right? Now, imagine that half is divided into six segments, each 30 degrees wide. Move your eyes from the far left segment to the far right segment and then repeat it several times. Notice the play of light against the trees and branches. If you move your head faster each time, your imagination will take over and those trees, with their odd shapes and eerie light and shadows, come to life. Now imagine what you would see if there is less light, perhaps only moonlight."

"It's scary, Buck," said Erika, pointing at a particular tree. "I was sure that the dark tree over there moved like the shadow of a bear standing up and waving his arms. Only his grunt or growl was missing."

Buck said with a smile, "I'll bear that in mind."

"Both of you are barely right. But it's more than scary," said Marlene. "It's downright terrorizing. Perhaps Max was frightened and thought he saw a bear coming at him from the woods when it was his imagination gone wild."

As they started back to the farmhouse, six of Max's Trakehners appeared, all spread out in a line between Tannenbaums. They pawed the ground with their hooves and whinnied, over and over, until the echoes faded away.

After the trio settled into the farmhouse, Marlene called the police and gave them all the information about Max's death. Ten minutes later the telephone rang: it was the police advising her that they were on their way to investigate the situation.

Buck then telephoned Winkelstüberl and asked the proprietor to free up his room and hold his suitcase until he returned the next morning to pay his bill.

CHAPTER 4

A n hour later, as dusk was approaching, an ambulance followed by a Mercedes sedan came up the driveway and parked in front of the garage.

Felix Chipmann, a towering six-foot, six-inch slender man, introduced himself as head of the Homicide Bureau of rural Munich, Federal Criminal Police Office of Germany, known as *Bundeskriminalamt*, abbreviated BKA.

"My office covers the southern portion of Bavaria, centered in Munich, and is the German version of the FBI in your country," he told Buck.

Chipmann then handed Marlene his name card and asked her to lead him and his team to the deceased and to be careful not to disturb the death scene.

Marlene obliged and guided everyone across the meadow into the woods then pointed to the body of her husband. Four others on Chipmann's team spread out and took notes and hundreds of photographs. One member of the team used a paint-spray can to outline the deceased's body.

By six o'clock Max's body and the bear trap were placed inside a body bag and loaded into the ambulance.

Ernst Schwartz, Felix's assistant and a peewee of a man when compared physically to his boss--but one of the brightest investigators in the bureau--picked up something resembling a small lump of coal. He used his left hand to get an idea of its weight.

The Inspector caught a glimpse of his action and asked, "What do you have there?"

"Too light to be a stone or lump of coal," Ernst told him then pressed it to his nose. "Smells fruity!"

"Sometimes I think all of you are a little fruity," bellowed Chipmann. "I guess it goes with the job and territory."

"Bear shit, I presume," answered Ernst.

"You mean spat?" asked Chipmann.

"Huh?"

"Bear shit is called spat," Chipmann answered. "Remind me to assign you to the veterinarian lab so you can learn the difference between animals of the forest and their eating habits. If you're going to work in rural areas, it would help if you know bear shit from cow shit."

"Dung."

"Huh?"

"Cow shit is called dung or pats, pies, or manure," answered Ernst. "I'm not as dumb as you think I am but maybe a short stint in the veterinarian lab would help."

He then tossed the lump over his shoulder where it landed close to the trunk of the giant oak tree.

"You know, before you toss me into the pool of mentally deficient detectives," continued Ernst, "remember that some rascally forest animals love to eat wild berries, so it is logical their spat would smell fruity, right?"

Chipmann asked for permission to interview Buck, Marlene, and Erika at the farmhouse, otherwise they would be compelled to travel to Munich the next morning.

"It is important," he told them, "actually vital, to get information from you while it is fresh. I apologize for prolonging your grief, but time and accuracy are of the essence here."

Once everyone was comfortable inside the farmhouse, Chipmann began by explaining that it appeared that Max was not killed by a bear.

"But we cannot rule out the possibility that Max may have been frightened by the roar of a bear nearby," Chipmann told them. "We found no bear tracks anywhere within 50 meters of his body. The question that puzzles me is why would he be in that spot in the first place? Forgive me for asking, did you know anyone who may have harbored a grudge against Max and sought revenge?"

Chipmann's notebook computer was placed in a position nearby to record every word that followed his opening remarks. Marlene was quick on the uptake and mentioned customers who bought his horses for export.

"I was never allowed to be present when he entertained clients in his lab. Although I kept his books for accounting purposes, it was forbidden for me to be around whenever he had appointments with clients. Their identity was considered top secret. I suspect that one or more of them may have had a bearing on his death."

She then switched tracks and confessed a few details about mistreatment by her husband; mistreatment that she considered bullying and mental cruelty. Her confession lasted about three minutes.

"I guess you can add my name to the top of your list of suspects," she concluded to Chipmann. "But let me make this perfectly clear: although I may have had a motive by often hoping that he would pass into another world, I would never, ever attempt to take anyone's life, especially that of Max, my husband."

Erika quickly followed up her Mother's lead with, "And you can put me next on your list, Herr Chipmann. It's no secret that I often hoped he would catch a bad case of influenza and would disappear and leave no traces of his existence.

"My mother tried to protect me, but, by the expression on her face, she evidently didn't realize the full extent of his mistreatment of me, too."

Marlene and Erika rushed to embrace one another, and each wiped away tears that streamed down their cheeks.

Buck watched the cuckoo emerge from its doorway in a second cuckoo clock; this one was an elaborately hand-carved Black Forest clock positioned in the middle of the wall. After it cooed the 10 o'clock hour, he summarized his experiences when facing Max earlier in the day and had mixed feelings about his tormentor's shocking ending in a bear trap.

"Although I wanted to take revenge," confessed Buck, "I would never go so far as to inflict any harm on a human being. I don't need to kill anyone; that would not help me be better than I am."

Chipmann realized everyone was exhausted from the ordeal and decided to halt the proceedings. "Thank you all for your indulgence and testimony. I can't wait to receive the coroner's report," he told them, "and I will meet with you again as soon as possible with an update of his findings."

Early the next morning Buck drove the pickup truck to Winkelstüberl. After returning his bike to Tutz, the owner of the rental bike concession, he paid his bill at the Inn and retrieved his luggage. As he was leaving, he recognized the odor that can come only from a bakery and its freshly baked cakes and pies. He followed his nose to the nearby display cases of the carryout counter. As he slowly walked there, he studied the framed certificates hanging on the wall. Each told something important about the history of this Inn that dated back to 1300 when Hans Winkle first opened his café for business.

By now Buck could not resist the temptation to slip into paradise, and he bought an assortment of specialties to enhance Max's wake. His selections included Schwarzwalder kirschetorte, Bayerische vanillecremetorte, Hollander kirschetorte, Mailander apfelschnitte, and apfelstrudel.

Before leaving, Buck telephoned Rudi Hofstedler and informed him that he would not be joining the group for the planned visit to Oktoberfest. He explained quickly that something important compelled him to stay a bit longer in the area, but he hoped that they would meet again. Lastly, Buck gave Hofstedler Marlene Allesin's phone number as a backup in case anyone needed him.

About an hour later, inside the farmhouse at Fischbachau, Marlene, Erika, and Buck were relaxed and enjoying a coffee klatch of sorts with the tortes purchased from Winkelstüberl. It was a somewhat abnormal wake for the newly departed and mentally disgruntled Mad Max but who cared? The goodies that were set out spotlighted the remarkable talents of Josef Mairhofer who took over Winkelstüberl in 1950 (it was now run by his daughter Thekla). Each product was like a masterpiece, a *pièce de résistance* with its unique design and taste, all the result of Mairhofer's training in Berlin. Each piece was fit for an Empress, a Kaiser, a Baron, or a Prince.

"You haven't mentioned once about your poison ivy itch," Marlene said to Buck while savoring a cherry torte.

"With the chain of events leading up to this moment, who cares about an itch?" Buck laughed. "If I had an itch, it would be to taste every one of Mairhofer's creations. My taste buds are dancing to a jazzy polka with Art van Damme on the accordion!"

"Life can be an itch not easily scratched," Erika said.

"What a prophetic statement from a 21-year old," said Buck.

"Out of the mouth of a baby like me comes wisdom," said Erika. "Actually, I cannot take credit for that statement. I read it or heard it many years ago and stored it away for such an occasion as this."

"What other gems do you have stored away in your warehouse?" asked Buck.

"You'll have to find that out for yourself when we're alone," Erika answered with a flirty grin.

About 30 minutes later the sounds of a roaring motor car with its tires grinding into the gravel road were heard through an open window. The car screeched to a halt, followed by a knocking on the front door. It was Inspector Chipmann, who asked them to take a seat and make themselves as comfortable as possible.

"Yesterday, I was suspicious about your confessing no intent to take Max's life, despite the presence of your footprints around his body," said Chipmann. "Perhaps, that was an indication that you were there before he died and not after, as you have claimed. However, the coroner's report was handed to me earlier this morning. Analysis of Max's corpse confirmed the time of his demise to be yesterday around 5 PM, which means all of you were away from the death scene. According to your testimony, Marlene and Erika were busy in the kitchen, and Buck was standing nude as nude can be on their doorstep."

"So, what are you saying about accusations and motives? Are we no longer suspects?" asked Marlene.

"If we are still suspects, you're barking up the wrong Tannenbaum, Inspector," said Buck.

Chipmann chuckled, paused, and asked for a glass of water.

"I heard the water around here is the best in Bavaria, perhaps from a virgin spring, right?"

"How about a shot of schnapps." Marlene said. "It's recommended by doctors to steady your nerves."

The Inspector walked around the room then stomped both feet on the wood floor, so hard that the sounds echoed off the walls and sent a chill up everyone's back.

"Forgive me, but I love to get the feel of the solid construction of these old houses that were built like fortresses. So, in keeping with solid construction, up to now I have been following protocol and guidelines for investigation of a homicide. I was compelled to document your statements on the death of Max Allesin. You know how German bureaucracy is inclined to fill records and notebooks to show that no stone is left untouched."

Chipmann saw a comfortable empty chair, settled into it, and said, "I'll have that shot of schnapps now, please."

"So, are we no longer suspects?" asked Marlene.

"That is correct, but as I said before this case is far from over."

By this time everyone was exhausted and ready for bed. That is, everyone except Marlene. After Chipmann and his team left the farmhouse, she asked Buck and Erika to have a seat at the dinner table. She pulled out her handkerchief, slowly and meticulously opened it, and placed it in the center of the table.

"This is something special that will make your sleep more restful tonight. Can you tell me what it is?"

"My guess is if it looks like bear spat, smells fruity like bear spat, and is light like bear spat, then it's bear spat, right?" said Buck.

"Wrong," said Marlene.

Erika picked up the lump, brought it closer to her eyes and nose and said, "A vegetable like a radish, horseradish, sugar beet, maybe?"

You are looking at something that sells for 3,000 euros a kilogram," said Marlene. "It is worth more than gold!"

"Well, it is past my bed time and no time to play games," said Buck. "I don't know about Erika, but I wish you wouldn't keep us in suspense any longer."

"It is a truffle," said Marlene with a devilish grin. "When I saw the way that it rolled on the ground almost to the trunk of the oak tree, I remembered something the friar told me when he was here a few years ago. He said that his frock was caught on a low oak branch as he was meandering through the woods near that oak tree. He looked carefully around the oak as he managed to free his frock, and he saw the mother lode. I asked him, 'Mother lode of what?', but he just grinned and told me to find that answer myself and that the answer would bring me a pot of gold."

<hr />

The next morning Marlene escorted everyone, including Chipmann and his team, across the meadow to the base of the mountain to search Max's laboratory. It was located in a small abandoned salt mine. There were no windows to let in fresh air or sunlight. It was constructed more than 20 years ago in a way that was as up-to-date as possible.

The lab had plenty of ducts for ventilation plus a sprinkler system in case of a fire. The counters were filled with distillation bottles, electronic equipment, and glass tubing running in all directions. Boxes and bottles of assorted sizes filled the inside cabinets that surrounded the walls. The area resembled a pharmacy more than a laboratory.

Under the supervision of Chipmann, everyone spent the next two days going over Max's journals, correspondence files, and notes pertaining to his experiments with breeding horses.

"Let me make this perfectly clear at the outset," said Marlene to Chipmann. "You can see from the handwriting in all the account books and daily journals that there are only two handwritings, mine and Max's. He was paranoid about leaving me alone inside or about my knowing anything of the people he contacted and permitted into his lab."

"Why was that?" asked Chipmann.

"My guess is… protection and security. If anything went haywire, I would not be held responsible."

"Did you ever see any of the people he let into his lab?"

"Only from a distance and by accident. I would not be qualified to identify anyone in a police lineup or scan of photographs."

Buck and Erika tried to keep from giving the police any notion of their being considered conspirators or being a participant in Max's business. Instead, they had their own agenda and tried hard to make their attraction to one another as discrete as possible. However, Marlene was well aware of Buck's growing interest in her daughter and seemed to encourage the beginning of their romance. She noticed that Buck seemed to make it a common practice that, when Erika found something for Chipmann to review, he congratulated her by putting his arm around her and whispering into her ear. Buck had a gleam in his eyes as his heart skipped a beat.

Buck noticed an entry in the files he was studying with the heading "Encapsulation Hermetically Sealed" followed by the letters "CC."

Marlene told him those letters could mean "See Computer."

"But I see no computer in the lab," Buck responded quickly.

"Max kept it inside his safe for security," said Marlene. "I believe we can find someone to open it. It's an old safe with a combination lock."

Chipmann told her that one of his staff was qualified to open the safe.

Ten minutes later the safe was opened. The first thing they saw inside was Max's laptop computer. They moved it to his desk in a far corner of the lab. Everyone huddled around Marlene as she tried repeatedly to gain access with Max's password.

"He was the only one permitted to use the laptop computer," she told them. "He was paranoid about secrecy. I remember asking him about his will and whether his daughter and wife were listed as beneficiaries. I told him he couldn't take anything with him when he died. He sneered and answered, 'No, I cannot take it with me, but I am the only one who knows my access code and I *can* take that with me!'"

"Maybe we will get lucky if we begin to think like Max and find it out," said Erika. "Thank God, by the looks of the age of his computer, we don't need his fingerprint for access."

Several hours of labor followed and frustration grew deeper. Finally, Erika suggested "Trakehner4Max."

Marlene typed it into the computer, and it worked. All of Max's files were now available for viewing. The files revealed that he implanted a microchip of data into the mane of his Trakehners that were scheduled for export to the Royal Saudi Family.

The files also disclosed that Max had devised a method to encapsulate the chip so that, once implanted, the casing would dissolve after precisely 10 days. If a horse was quarantined longer than 10 days, the chip would be ruined and all the data would disappear. Consequently, Max specified in each contract that the buyer was responsible for removing the chip within 10 days maximum, and he would not be liable for any mishaps or losses.

"I think that Max was mad, all right," Marlene mused. "He

seemed to have been a mad, but brilliant, veterinarian with a very distorted view of life."

"I agree with you," Erika said sadly.

"It appears as though much of his work was criminal – and done with criminal intent," Marlene said. "I'm sure his intention – and the impulse – behind his crimes was to make big money fast."

"Marlene, you have a big brain behind your beautiful head," said Buck.

"You're right on the money, Mom," said Erika.

"Like mother, like daughter," said Buck. "You also have great intelligence inside that beautiful head."

When Marlene attempted to put the computer back into the safe, she noticed a stack of money that was barely visible. The cash amounted to more than one hundred thousand euros, none of which was freshly minted.

"It must have accumulated over at least 10 years," said Marlene. "And I thought Max was a poor farmer and vet."

"Maybe now we can hire a cook and butler," Erika said, "and have a party catered by Winkelstüberl."

CHAPTER 5

Felix Chipmann nodded to his assistant to step forward. "Perhaps this is as good a time as ever to introduce you formally to my assistant, Ernst Schwartz, Chief of Detectives. Don't let his size fool you. He is a master of Metaphysics, a branch of philosophy that explores the nature of concepts, such as cause and effect, space and time…ah…what is reality, existence, and being. It tries to answer the question of 'What is there and what is it like,' just like Kant wrote it many years ago."

Ernst Schwartz was a five-foot, six-inch, overweight, and wimpy-looking man standing beside his slender six-foot, six-inch boss, who often was called "the lanky one" of the administration. But Schwartz had something his boss didn't, namely a medal on his lapel testifying to his 25-year career for the Bureau. He essentially and intentionally remained in the background like a fly on the wall. Now he stepped forward with supreme confidence and began to study the faces of everyone in the room carefully. Then Schwartz turned on the video camera to record everything said from this moment forward.

"First," said Schwartz, "some of you will be surprised to learn that we have been monitoring Max for the past five years. He came to our attention because we found it unusual for a German who started as a farmer growing sunflowers and hops to quickly turn into a veterinarian who sold Trakehners to an export agent representing the Royal Saudi Family. The income from the production of crops was not that substantial, but the income from the Trakehners was very substantial."

"You knew about Max that long," asked Marlene, "without me knowing more about the details of his business? He really kept us in the dark, didn't he?"

"We began to monitor Max's activities," answered Schwartz, "using cameras with high definition images and recordings, both inside and outside the salt mine. Max felt someone was spying on him and was right. We tapped phone lines, monitored movements in and out of Fischbachau, and concentrated on everyone that he came in contact with. As for Max, we even knew from his hospital records that he had fallen backward on a sheet of ice 18 years ago and was hospitalized."

Schwartz continued to describe this accident when Max was rushing to get his Trakehners across the meadow and into their shed for protection from the windy snowfall.

"Then – when we first started monitoring Max - we saw him slip on something on his lab floor and fall backward and crack his head.

"Although he was hospitalized, the attending physicians never performed any tests for a possible concussion. Now we know that this accident could have contributed to the beginning of Chronic Traumatic Encephalopathy, which would account for his change in behavior.

"CTE is a brain disease, perhaps not exactly a disease but more like a condition, resulting from repeated injuries to the head. We know that his headaches affected his thinking, and he had personality changes that were frequent and increasing in intensity. His memory problem, lack of control of his impulses, and behavior changes including depression and aggression were becoming more pronounced and violent. CTE, you must remember here, is not easily manifested. It may occur months, years, even decades after an injury.

"A definitive diagnosis may be achieved only when an autopsy is performed and a forensic neuropathologist analyzes the brain for evidence of a concussion. And here is one final point before closing this issue. Repeated blows to the head may not cause unconsciousness but will increase the risk of CTE."

Felix interrupted Schwartz to show a short clip from one of the surveillance cameras of Max at the break of dawn in his barn tending to one of his Trakehners. In the dimly lit aisle he was engaged in examining the horse's mane.

Max mumbled indistinctly to himself while he checked the horse's suitability for having a microchip inserted under its mane.

Suddenly, the silence inside the barn was shattered by a massive clap of thunder and a tremendous bolt of lightning that struck nearby. An intermittent failure of electric power and blinking lights in the barn increased the tension.

A hooded crow resting in the rafters was aroused from his perch and stretched his black head and beak above his ash-grey plumage. The crow then swooped down into the aisle of the barn as if in slow motion because of its heavy weight. As it approached Max and his horse, the crow cawed in a freakish voice and flapped his wings so violently that the horse spooked and swung his rear end toward Max with a force that lifted Max off his feet and tossed him against the wall.

Max lost consciousness as a result of hitting his head. The force was enough to undoubtedly cause a concussion.

About an hour later Marlene found Max a little groggy and, when asked what happened, he could not remember anything except the lightning strike.

Schwartz then explained that the coroner's report showed undeniable evidence from an MRI and CAT scan of Max's brain that he had a significant growth of malignant tissue. "This discovery probably accounted for his increased belligerence and abuse to everyone he came in contact with. That must have been, pardon the expression, hell for his family to bear."

Marlene removed a handkerchief from a pocket and wiped some tears from her eyes and from Erika's. "I had no idea what was behind his actions. I thought it was something I failed to do or worse yet, did to him unknowingly."

Schwartz paused to inhale a deep breath. "We still don't know exactly the reason why, but Max became a traitor to Germany, his homeland. We don't know whether it was the desire for money or power or whether it was disenchantment with Germany and its ever-increasing government control. But he was susceptible and probably easily enticed to enter into an agreement with a foreign agent named Cal."

Schwartz explained that Cal's real name was Khalid Najjar Khalid, who was born in Germany, the oldest of three sons of Yemeni parents. "Khalid means eternal or immortal or everlasting, and Najjar means Carpenter, ironically the occupation of Jesus's earthly father."

"This is growing more suspenseful minute by minute," said Marlene.

At this point Buck turned white and muttered to himself, "Oh, my God, that's the man who was on the train with us." Buck started to say something, but Schwartz was still talking, and Buck did not want to interrupt him.

"You haven't heard anything yet," Schwartz said. "Permit me to go on a bit longer, please. When Max first met Cal, Max treated him as simply a coffee buyer with a penchant for importing Trakehners to Saudi Arabia. I doubt if Max knew much more because he certainly would not have been told initially by Cal about his connection as a foreign agent of ISIS. But at some point, Max surely knew that his insertion of a chip with critical information for ISIS into the mane of his Trakehners was an illegal act and came with some risk and criminal liability."

Schwartz went on to explain how Max first met Cal at the Oktoberfest about four years ago. "We had agents tracking Max everywhere he went, day and night. Over this period, we learned that this agent was not the only one purchasing horses from Max. Each year Max had at least three buyers of his Trakehners. But Cal was the only one buying them and transporting them to the Saudi Royal Family."

Buck could stay quiet no longer; he rose from his chair and said, "I did not know any of this. He told everyone in the compartment that he was born in Germany but his parents were Yemeni. That was after I noticed his Arabic newspaper and mentioned it to him. That's about all I can remember. Oh, yes, he also said that he was importing coffee from Yemen and had a rendezvous with a breeder of horses."

"To reiterate," said Schwartz, "After Cal met Buck, shortly before their train arrived in Munich Central Station, Cal then rented a car and eventually kept his rendezvous with Max. This meeting, like their others, was fairly routine. Cal always parked his car in the woods near Max's farm, telephoned Max that he was 10 minutes away, and then walked through the woods as quietly and discretely as possible to Max's lab."

"Max surely was an unpopular fellow, wasn't he," asked Buck.

"Not to ISIS he wasn't," interjected Schwartz.

Marlene wiped the perspiration from her brow and admitted, "The suspense is killing me, gentlemen, but I need to excuse myself. I'll be right back."

After Marlene returned to her seat, Schwartz continued to explain that once Cal was inside Max's lab, he would hand Max a microchip containing the names and pertinent information of farmers in Bayerische Oberland who agreed unknowingly to collaborate with ISIS by sponsoring exchange students from Saudi Arabia. Schwartz raised his voice and told them that the information on the microchip was encrypted and added to the data about the horse that already was on the microchip. The chip was then encapsulated and hermetically sealed by Max and implanted under the mane of a Trakehner destined for export.

"When the Trakehners arrived in Saudi Arabia," Schwartz said, "an ISIS agent posing as an assistant to the trainer for the Saudi

Royal Family stables, would remove the chip and pass it up the line to controllers for further processing. Eventually, the farmers became unwitting collaborators when they were assigned their students. I say, 'collaborator' because there is a difference between a sympathizer and a collaborator, and the difference is money.

"Each exchange student was recruited from Saudi Arabia and agreed to work in exchange for food, lodging, and training. For example, two students would study how the host farmer experimented with genetics of hops and barley used in the breweries. Another pair would study the genetics of rye to make liquor or would study robotics to process everything from picking to shipping. This was purely an acclamation period for the students with the prospect of eventually being ordered to commit a terrorist act."

"Would you mind if I had a shot of schnapps," asked Buck, "I need something to calm my nerves."

"Make one for me, too," Erika said emphatically. "How about you two?" Erika asked pointing to Chipmann and Schwartz.

"I make it a habit not to drink on the job unless I am desperate," answered Schwartz. "But today is an exception, so pour a double for me." He downed it quickly then continued. "I cannot guarantee that Max knew that these students might one day be ordered to fly a plane into the Reichstag or into a football stadium with 100,000 spectators. But Max must have known something because he constantly asked for more money to compensate him for the increased risk he was taking for his participation.

"In his defense I will confess that he may not have known what was encrypted on the microchip but he certainly could hazard a guess that it wasn't a poem by Schiller or the music to one of Richard Wagner's operas."

Schwartz ruffled a few papers inside his manila folder and told them that at this point Max was beginning to stir up too many feathers for Cal to bear.

"The point of contention mainly now was the money Max wanted for the increased risk and liability. He was becoming more irrational and erratic and Cal gradually lost confidence in Max's ability to remain silent and steadfast. Because of his constant confrontation, Cal felt Max could slip up, go berserk, and inadvertently say something about the organization that was intolerable and destructive."

"At some point in the afternoon of the day Max died," said Chipmann, "we know from monitors inside his lab that Max argued with Cal and asked him bluntly, 'Do you really want to know what bugs me most about dealing with you?'"

Chipmann then told everyone to bear with him while he put his laptop computer on the table so everyone could see the video replay of Max's and Cal's conversation. It began with Cal answering Max's question.

"If it makes you happier," said Cal reluctantly as Chipmann increased the volume, "proceed, Counselor."

"It is my gut feeling that you don't respect me," said Max. "You forget that I love my Trakehners from the time they are born, even before they are born. Each one has its own personality. It is not just a Trakehner that you buy, it is a Max Trakehner. The way I crossbreed with Arabian horses, I pour my heart and soul and energy into each one to make it the best one of its breed. Can you begin to understand what I'm talking about? That's mainly why I am asking for more money from you."

"You always said it was compensation for the increased risk you were taking."

"Yes, but I want a lake house and townhouse to go with my farmhouse, a place where I can relax and get lost...a retreat...a getaway where I can find a cure for my migraine headaches that are increasing in frequency and intensity."

"What you need is a protector, someone to look after you better, like me," offered Cal facetiously.

"I have my protector right here," answered Max, opening his lab coat and pointing to the pistol in his shoulder holster. "My Glock G46 is my protector."

Max patted the holster fondly. "Glocks are used by the German police," he said. "They call it their *glockenspiel*, because it is music to their ears."

Marlene said apologetically in a voice slightly above a whisper to no one in particular, "I can't believe this is the man that I fell in love with and who became the father of my girl."

At this point Schwartz froze the video replay and explained that Max was further infuriated by Cal's failure to give him time to prepare his horses for their implant. Cal seemed bent on antagonizing Max with a push and a rush to meet nearly impossible ISIS commitments.

Chipmann fast forwarded through the tape, adding that Cal was patient when he felt Max was forcing a showdown by asking for more pay or else. Then Cal surprised Max when he told him that Max's problems might be solved sooner than he thought.

"Look what happened next," Chipmann said, pressing PLAY.

"You pike," Max called Cal.

"Insulting an agent in the exercise of his duties may be cause to cease and desist our relationship," Cal said. "Did you mean kike?"

"No, I meant what I said. Pike, a carnivorous fish that eats weaker ones – bit by bit."

"Spare me the fishing lesson, please," Cal said. "This is no time to lose your temper. I could call you a 'hot head' and a 'hypocritical hypocrite,' but I won't stoop to your level and get into name-calling. Let's get back to what I told you a few moments ago; namely, that your problems might be solved sooner than you think."

"How…when?" asked Max.

"Starting with our next deal, if there's going to be a deal," said Cal, "you have to remember that you are only one of many breeders who presently infuse Arabian blood into their line of Trakehners."

"Obviously you know something that I don't, so spit it out…It doesn't look as if I will buy my retreat any time soon…not without putting a financial strain on my bank account."

"It appears that you have little choice," said Cal, "unless you make a sacrifice. Everyone, especially you, my friend, must make a sacrifice for the good of the team."

"In effect, the trainer has given me -- and I hereby pass along to you -- an ultimatum: meet our goals and schedules or..."

"No other options?"

"Yes, there is an alternative. My Saudi clients are keen to buy paintings of Arabian horses by the great 19ᵗʰ century German artist Adolf Schreyer. While he was alive, his works were collected by the richest American millionaires from Carnegie to Mellon. A number of his paintings are still available for purchase from galleries, auction houses, and private collectors around the world. It would be easy for you to implant your microchip into the stretcher bars of his paintings. In other words, we are switching your implant from horses to paintings. We will continue to use your services but without the need for your Trakehners."

"You seem to hold all the marbles in your hand," Max said, trying to play for time as he thought of a painting that was on a wall in his daughter Erika's room. It showed Arabian horsemen riding their magnificent steeds in a rocky landscape. He wondered if it was by the artist that Cal wanted; and he wondered how he could get his daughter to part with it if, indeed, it was by the right artist.

"We're not talking about marbles. We're talking about encapsulation and implants."

By this time Max was fit to be tied. His frustration grew into rage and he threw a large glass beaker filled with sulfuric acid against the wall and watched the cloud of fumes eat into the salt wall. He then grabbed Cal by the lapels of his suit.

As Cal's spectacles clouded with perspiration, he told Max to cool off unless he wanted to end their association for good. "This is not the time to be hot-headed," Cal told him emphatically.

Chipmann then directed an associate to turn off the monitor. He then told his audience, "We don't know what happened next; that is, how Max was found with his head encased in the bear trap.

But Ernst has an interesting and, I must admit, a good and plausible theory."

"In all probability, Cal had a plan in mind if his relations with Max became unbearable," Schwartz told them. "To say that things had reached the boiling point may be an understatement, as you will soon see.

"According to the video recordings, after Max ushered Cal into his lab, Max took a seat and pondered a way to convince him of a way to get their relationship back on track. However, he was interrupted by Cal who told him, 'This is the precise time to make a toast to our new relationship. There is nothing better than the taste of the medicinal benefits of Unterberger. It's good for whatever ails you!'

"Let's look at the monitor again and you can see the rest for yourselves."

Max at first resisted taking alcohol and explained that he still had a chip to encapsulate. "You should be aware, if you are not already, that contradictions make me fearless, expectations drive me to higher heights."

Cal, however, ignored Max and his outburst. He ordered him to remain seated and take a load off his mind, then he went to a cabinet, removed a bottle of Unterberger liquor, and poured two shots in a glass, one for each of them.

"Unterberger will cure your ills. Let's raise our glasses in a toast not just to a new and better relationship. It is a toast to change," said Cal, grabbing Max's shoulders so that he remained seated in his swivel chair.

When they finished their toast, Max realized that, despite Cal's toast, nothing had changed between them. This was a death knell notice that resounded like bells ringing in Max's brain.

Max was infuriated, probably from the effects of the liquor, and grabbed Cal by the lapels on his dress suit. "I don't believe you have the right respect for me."

"Forgive me for repeating myself again, but being a hot head will not get us over the hurdles facing us," said Cal.

Max admitted his mistake but stubbornly never apologized.

"Without Max being aware of it, it appeared as though Cal now became a predator and demanded they make another toast to the past, present, and future," Chipmann told his audience and returned to the recording.

"All for one and one for all," Cal shouted as he refilled the shot glasses. Only this time he slipped a Mickey Finn with a deluxe spin into Max's glass. The capsule was the date-rape drug Rohypnol, which was guaranteed to incapacitate a victim and render him vulnerable to whatever a predator had in mind.

Cal blocked the light so Max would not notice the color change of the liquor from a Burgundy red to a cloudy Rembrandt burnt sienna.

At this point, Max was still coherent and asked for his cash payment. Cal searched his pockets and although he had the money on him, told Max he probably left the envelope in the briefcase inside his rental car. Max was then persuaded to walk with Cal through the forest as rain began to fall.

As they watched the recording, Chipmann and his rapt audience may not have been surprised at what happened next.

Five minutes later Max began to hallucinate a little and lose control of his muscles, especially those in his legs.

Max's vision played tricks on his mind as he started to see movement in the trees and was convinced that a large bear was moving toward him and ultimately standing upright with its head high and arms outstretched. Max looked at the bear and giggled that the bear didn't scare him because he looked so far away and so bedraggled from the rain.

Max begged for a short pause and rested on the fallen rotted tree trunk. When Max dropped his head to his chest, Cal walked up behind him and, just as lightning erupted nearby, Cal struck Max on the back of his head with a heavy blow from the butt of his handgun. Cal then grabbed Max's shoulder and pulled him backward, dragging him about ten feet and placing Max's head inside the large bear trap. Max never knew what hit him.

As Schwartz prepared to continue with his presentation Chipmann interjected, "The coroner said in his report that Max may have died from the blow to the back of his head, or from the clamping action of the bear trap, or both."

Suddenly, over the lab's stereophonic audio system a recording of Richard Wagner's *Valkyrie* blared out of the speakers with a force that literally lifted everyone out of their chairs.

"I would have preferred *Tristan and Isolde*," said Marlene. "That was Max's time clock to close up for the day. He rarely worked past 1600 hours."

"Another eccentricity of Max, I presume," said Schwartz.

Marlene asked nervously, "Herr Schwartz, where in the hell does that leave us now?"

"I'm about to tell you," Schwartz told them and paused to clear his throat. "At this time, we, meaning the homicide bureau, want each of you to continue doing whatever you intended to do each hour of each day. Marlene, keep paying his bills like the telephone, Internet, and accounts payable for lab equipment. We will monitor Max's contacts as if he died of an accident. Buck can produce his story with photos if he wants to, but I would advise against it… unless you want a steady stream of busy bees trampling over this beautiful land and asking lots of questions and taking up much of your time."

"What about the exchange students?" asked Buck. "You didn't tell us what happened to them. Did they return to Saudi Arabia? We know that they did not hijack a plane, or did they?"

"For your information," answered Felix, "up through the end of last year, those students who had visas to work on farms totaled about 32 over a 4-year period. As far as we know, not one of those students has stayed in Germany beyond the permitted date when their visas expired. So far, according to our records, each has returned to Saudi

Arabia. But there are no current records that we can find of their being alive or deceased.

"Of course, they could have taken a new identity, or disappeared in the desert, or were assigned to a different cell under a new *nom de guerre*, a variant of their real name. Also, we do not yet have the statistics for anyone who has entered Germany on a student visa since the end of last year."

Schwartz again paused to wipe the moisture from inside his glasses. His face was covered in sweat and the stress of his talk had a big impact on his demeanor. "I wish we could feel comfortable and confident that none of those students who has studied here so far is an immediate threat to the security of Germany, but I am compelled to issue a disclaimer that I am not liable for anything I have said because as of now the intelligence gatherers who work under the auspices of the Justice Department have not been able to confirm where the students are or even whether they are alive or dead."

Finally, Erika closed the session by asking Schwartz, "What in the world would Cal have to gain when he was already a millionaire in the coffee business in Haraaz, Yemen? Why put your life on the line to join ISIS?"

"Good questions, young lady, for which I honestly don't have a good answer, except off the top of my head, I believe it was a lust for power and invincibility."

"Maybe Cal had a latent joy over seeing another person beheaded or his throat cut," said Buck. "Blood thirsty he could have been or wanting revenge for the chaos growing in Yemen." He paused and added, "Perhaps he wanted to be a billionaire and tap into the treasury of the Saudi Royal family."

The following morning Chipmann telephoned Marlene and asked her to arrange for Erika and Buck to join him and Schwartz in a conference call of vital importance as soon as possible. Marlene told him that they were all gathered together at this moment and ready to take that conference call.

Chipmann explained that overnight he came to the conclusion that everyone involved must now agree to enter into a phase of, for lack of a better name, damage control. He told them it was a first step, but a big step, in letting ISIS assume that Max died accidentally and that his operation would continue with Marlene taking charge. He offered no more details at this moment, except to tell them he was formulating a plan of action that would be forthcoming in a few days. He tried his best to explain the risk they were being asked to take.

Buck told him, "I have been waiting for an opportunity to pay back ISIS and honor my father and mother and the thousands of those who gave their lives on 9/11. The payback for 9/11 is worth more -- much more -- than the risk, don't you think?"

CHAPTER 6

T he next day Marlene received a follow-up phone call from Chipmann while she and Erika and Buck were finishing their breakfast in the great room of the farmhouse. He told them about the ISIS exchange students living and working for a farmer nearby, a farmer who, Chipmann was convinced, was unknowingly working to the advantage of ISIS. Chipmann told Marlene to keep her emotions on an even keel and to give him a progress report over the phone at precisely 8 PM each day.

When the conference call was concluded, Buck asked Marlene and Erika about an antique slant-top desk positioned in the middle of a wall near a window in his room.

"We had a reproduction in Hoboken," he told them. "My mother said she learned her lessons by reading and writing on the drop-down lid."

Marlene explained that it was an antique left by the previous owners when Max's parents bought the place lock, stock, and barrel.

Erika told him that she still used the desk to store correspondence. Buck asked them if they were aware of a secret compartment behind one of the drawers. Erika and Marlene were puzzled and intrigued by Buck's question.

"Let's go upstairs so I can show you instead of trying to explain it," Buck told them as he headed for the stairs. "I will remove the far-right drawer first and then the one next to it. Notice the far-right one measures about eight inches in length whereas the one next to it measures sixteen inches. What does that tell you?"

"I am embarrassed to tell you I haven't a clue why the two lengths are not the same," said Marlene.

"Are they supposed to be the same?" Erika asked. "Did the furniture maker run out of wood?"

"The mystery about the difference in lengths is explainable simply by pressing a button embedded on the bottom end of the eight-inch drawer," he told them. "Erika, look closely and push the button, please."

A slight click was heard and another drawer moved slightly toward Erika. She noticed an indentation in the front of this mystery drawer where she could take her fingernail and pull it forward. One could hear a pin drop in the sudden silence.

Marlene and Erika were both stunned. But then came a surprise and a shock. Inside the hidden drawer were photographs, some black and white, others in color, and some with notes written on the reverse side.

It took Buck only a few seconds to let out a howl and tell them some of these photos matched ones his mother had in her scrapbooks in Hoboken.

"This means that the desk was used by your mother and must have come from this house," said Marlene. "Moreover, you bear a striking resemblance to your mother in these photos. And the young girl reading to her family in the painting hanging in my bedroom bears a resemblance to your mother."

They rushed to Marlene's bedroom and there it was, the painting Buck's mother had described to him: the one that her father had bought at an estate sale in Schliersee because the girl in the painting reminded him of his daughter.

The Reading Lesson
Ludwig Vollmar

"How is it that you can remember so many details?" asked Erika.

"I may not be the world's best photographer but I have a memory for vital facts and formulas and trivia that astounded my professors at Lehigh," Buck admitted with confidence. "That is why they encouraged me to become a photojournalist."

Marlene examined the painting closely and told them it was signed "Ludwig Vollmar, Munchen."

"Oh, and look," Erika exclaimed as she examined more of the photos from the desk. "Here's a photo of a painting that is in my room. I did some research and discovered it is by a German painter names Adolf Schreyer who is famous for painting Arabian horses better than any other artist in his time."

Arab Horsemen in a Mountainous Landscape
Adolf Schreyer

Marlene excused herself by telling them that she had some work to do in the lab. She advised Buck and Erika to relax by listening to the music of the oldies on the cassettes in the great room bookcase.

"These cassettes were left in the house when Max's father bought the property," Marlene explained.

"I heard the recordings so often and joined in," Erika told Buck. "My mother recognized my natural gift for singing as a vocation and thought of sending me to a conservatory to study voice. I became enamored with the words and music of the 1940s and 1950s because they were so full of meaning and feeling."

"Did you take her up on studying music?" Buck asked.

"My father was enraged when he heard of it and made a move to strike my behind but I was too quick and ran out of the house. He could be myopic at times."

"I assume you mean to say he was short-sighted and

narrow-minded. He may have deterred you from being another Vera Lynn or Dinah Shore, but if your mind tells you to study music at the academy, do it. Your future is now, not in the past. Don't look back to the future."

Buck lightened the mood by asking Erika to play a game of "Sing, you Sinner, for your Wings to Heaven."

"Let's play for some reward for the winner," said Buck.

Erika said, "I cannot agree until you give me more details and conditions."

Buck told her, "I will give you the title of a song and you have to sing the words to the song."

Erika licked her lips, smiled, and told him, "Pick your best and let me have a go at it!"

"Do you agree that the loser is required to buy lunch at Winkelstüberl?" asked Buck.

"Put a euro in the jukebox and make your choice, sir," said Erika.

"My first choice," said Buck, "is most appropriate for this moment in time. The title is *At Last.*"

"Can you give me a hint such as the names of the lyricist and composer?" Erika asked with a tinge of guilt since she knew a good deal about this song.

"The lyrics were written by Mack Gordon and music by Harry Warren," Buck said with pride.

Erika coughed to clear her throat and started to give some details about the biography of the lyricist and composer. She told Buck that the song was written in 1941. In a flurry she continued to add that both names were not their original family names. She told Buck that Harry Warren's real name was Salvador Antonio Guaragna, born in 1893, one of 11 children of an Italian bootmaker who gave his son accordion lessons. Mack Gordon was born Morris Gittler in 1904 in Warsaw, Poland, which was then part of the Russian Empire.

Buck presumed that he had lost the bet here but couldn't resist telling her, "I didn't ask for a bio. I asked you to sing the song -- period."

Erika smiled and started to sing the song slowly with each word pronounced with a special meaning and intonation.

> *At last my love has come along*
> *My lonely days are over and life is like a song.*
> *At last the skies above are blue*
> *My heart was wrapped in clover the night I looked*
> *at you.*
> *I found a dream that I can speak to*
> *A dream that I can call my own.*
> *I found a thrill to press my cheek to*
> *A thrill I've never known.*
> *Song: At Last - Ella Fitzgerald*

When it was Erika's turn to stump Buck with a song, she chose the ballad "You'll Never Know."

Buck smiled and knew he had evened the score. He lifted her out of her chair, put his hands on her shoulders, and sang the song with great feeling.

> *You'll never know just how much I miss you,*
> *You'll never know how much I care,*
> *And if I tried I still couldn't hide my love for you,*
> *Haven't I told you a million or more times.*
> *You went away and my heart went with you,*
> *I speak your name in my every prayer.*
> *Song: You'll Never Know - Vera Lynn*

He ended with more of the song, "*If there is some other way to tell you I love you, I swear I don't know how. You'll never know if you don't know now.*"

Erika answered, "I knew it the moment my heart skipped a beat when you suddenly appeared in the doorway without any clothes on, except for your sunglasses and hat, two days and nine hours ago."

They embraced and exchanged kisses for what seemed like an eternity.

"What are you doing?" Erika asked him.

"If you don't know, I must be doing something wrong," Buck told her and studied her smiling face a long time. "Isn't there something else you would like to ask me?"

Erika answered, "Yes. Where's the beef?"

Buck chuckled and realized that Erika was Americanized, knew about commercials on television, and was blessed with a good sense of humor. For him, nothing beat a good sense of humor.

Erika leaned her head on his shoulder and, with a mischievous grin, told him that she would like to give him a kiss but she was not sure she knew him well enough. This drew a laugh from Buck and he confessed to not knowing a lot about her but something inside told him that she was the girl for him.

Erika confessed that while she may not know enough about him, something inside told her that he was the man for her. She whispered slowly with feeling that he reminded her of Michelangelo's *David*. Before he could answer, she started to sing softly in his ear another Sinatra recording, "I Hadn't Anyone 'til You," with words and music by Ray Noble. She only sang the first four lines:

> *I hadn't anyone 'til you,*
> *I was a lonely one 'til you,*
> *I used to lie awake and wonder if there could be*
> *A someone in this wide world just made for me and*
> *now I see.*
> "I Hadn't Anyone Till You" - Frank Sinatra

Without his realizing it, Erika was leading Buck in a slow dance around chairs and tables. Finally, Buck stopped in his tracks and whispered into her ear, "David wooed Bathsheba with his harp but I am no David, and I never studied the harp. It seems that roles are reversed and you, like Bathsheba, have struck a chord deep in my heart with your song. I think I am falling in love."

Erika stopped singing and asked, "When will you know for sure?"

A broad smile covered her face and her eyes sparkled. "When will you know you're *in love*?"

"Huh?"

"When will you be certain?"

"I've always wanted someone I could give kisses to for breakfast… kisses to for lunch…kisses to for dinner…and…"

"And?"

"At night, a *roll* in the hay."

"Then I'm your someone."

"Yes, it's you. Friends said that I was indecisive, but now I'm not so sure," answered Buck with a stutter. "I'm beginning to feel numbness in my feet."

Erika paused and told him, "That's not the way it's supposed to work. Yea, God, it's been a long day. Speaking of feet, my feet are killing me."

Buck answered quickly, "You mean my feet are killing you, with missteps. I assure you that I can do much better on a proper dance floor."

"If that's an invitation for a date, I'll hold you to it!"

Erika and Buck finally realized that Buck's mobile phone had rung at least eight times before he answered it. The caller identified himself as a farmer from the nearby Starnberger See.

Buck asked the farmer the reason for his call and learned he was given this telephone number by Cal. Buck instantly assessed that there was no time to check with government officials, and he needed to play the part of Cal's colleague. He unhesitatingly told the farmer that he was an advisor to the student exchange program and asked the nature of the call. It was a brazen step for Buck to take, but time was of the essence here.

The farmer introduced himself as Franz Funk who was contracted by Cal to train two exchange students who were suddenly acting strangely. He suspected they may be planning to flee Germany by hijacking a private jet aircraft. He could not answer for sure whether they planned a terrorist attack or were going to fly to a country and ask for asylum.

Buck asked for Funk's address and ordered him to secure any vehicles that the two exchange students could use to escape. At no time did Buck reveal his name to the farmer. Instead, he asked what kind and color of clothes the farmer was wearing and asked him to wait on the front doorstep of his farm for Buck's signal, a loud whistle, as Buck would be leaving within the hour to meet Funk at his farm.

Buck then called Inspector Chipmann, told him Chipmann's advice about damage control was prophetic because Buck had just received a frantic telephone call from a farmer near Starnberger See who was training two exchange students who may have ill intentions. The Inspector told Buck that he was right not to reveal his identity to anyone. Chipmann advised Buck to take down notes to remember everything Chipmann was about to tell him.

"No need to do that, Sir," answered Buck. "My professors at Lehigh said that I have a photographic memory, although it sometimes is undeveloped!"

Chipmann didn't catch the pun and told Buck that he should now pretend to be a colleague of Cal and a secret agent responsible for crisis control. He proceeded to warn Buck of the risk and danger and told him to arm himself with a gun and use it if he was threatened at any time.

Buck told Chipmann he was confident and reasonably qualified to carry out Chipmann's order. He stressed in the strongest words possible, "It is the least I could do to honor my mother and father and the thousands who gave up their lives on 9/11. Semper fi!"

"What did you say, Buck?"

"Semper fi, which is short for semper fidelis," he replied. "It's an expression credited to the Marines in which my father was a career officer. He said it often and proudly, always with a salute. It means 'Always loyal, Always faithful.'"

Buck completed the phone call by asking Chipmann to put all his orders in writing to prevent Buck being accused of acting on his own initiative. Buck ended their conversation by telling Chipmann that he would pay the farmer a visit within the hour and learn everything there was to know about the problem with the Starnberger See farmer and his exchange students. Buck then raised his arms upward and outward to stretch and prepare himself to meet the challenge ahead.

CHAPTER 7

I t took Buck about an hour to drive Max's pickup from Fischbachau to Franz Funk's Starnberger See farm. When his GPS indicated that he was less than half a mile away from the farmhouse, Buck pulled the truck off the dirt road, drove into a heavily wooded area, and parked the truck well hidden from view. He walked through a short section of woods until he came to a meadow facing the farmhouse.

Buck noticed an old man wearing a green Bavarian hat, gave a loud whistle, and waved him over to the fringe of the woods. When they met, Buck extended his hand to the old man whose hand was shaking so wildly that Buck had to squeeze it tightly.

"I'm Franz Funk," mumbled the old man nervously.

Franz's head and face were the spitting image of Otto Preminger, except Franz had curly red hair.

"Of course, you are," said Buck, smiling to put him at ease. "Who else would you be?"

Franz was panting and appeared out of breath. He squirmed and grabbed his Adam's apple, a chronic reaction whenever he was worried. He was so nervous that he pulled his hat so tightly down around his ears that he heard the stitches in the lining pop.

Buck put his arm around Franz to reassure him that Franz was right to telephone his contact. Buck assured Franz that he was part of Cal's team and was there to offer his service to study the problem and to find a solution that would be mutually agreeable to everyone. The two then walked about 100 meters through the woods and kidded each other about the high pitch of birds and crickets in a battle for who could chirp the loudest.

They soon came to a small clearing with an Alpine hut that often was used by campers and hunters. Once inside, Franz wasted no time in excitedly recounting how he entered the room of his two exchange students, Ali Shiptoshur and Ben Ladeen, who were acting strangely for the past two weeks. He opened his jacket and showed Buck an assortment of maps and notebooks that he found in the room that both students shared in the main house.

He told Buck that Ali and Ben were behaving in a manner far superior to the demeanor expected of students pursuing a career in agricultural research. Veins in Franz's neck began to surface then expanded and contracted as he surmised that the papers he found may be drawings and schematics that the students could use to escape the area and hijack a plane. This discussion between Franz and Buck went slowly at first and lasted more than an hour.

During his revelation Franz's eyes were tearing and his hands were shaking. His voice quavered nervously and erratically.

"How could I be so gullible," said Franz. "This was clearly a betrayal by individuals I took into my confidence."

Buck tried to get in a word or two to lessen the tension and realized that Franz was at the breaking point because of events involving his liaison officer Cal and the exchange students assigned to him to study and work at his farm.

With no malice of forethought Franz reiterated that he was suspicious from the time that the students first started to study and work because they were so skilled and intelligent.

"I never thought of barging into their room or interfering with their personal things," said Franz, "but they were part of the exchange student program and allowed to occupy a room under my roof and care. I considered them temporarily a part of my family."

"What kind of man would befriend you and later betray you?" Franz asked with anger in his voice.

"There are millions like that, my friend," said Buck. "The best known to me was Judas."

Tears began to emerge from Franz's eyes.

"Traitors are always looking out for themselves and for their gain, not for yours," Buck responded and pushed his Stetson further back on his head.

"Most of the time tension brings out the worst in a person's psyche," Franz answered. "All one has to do is think about the commandant and guards and their treatment toward the Jews in their concentration camps."

Buck acted cool and collected and explained that he had the time and know-how to work on this crisis from the get-go. Franz told Buck that it was imperative to find out if Cal knew about these renegade students and if Cal was complicit in their activities and part of a conspiracy with ISIS to plant young men posing as exchange students with Bavarian farmers. Franz made it crystal clear that he wanted to gather more evidence and facts before reporting everything to the police.

This was a turning point for Buck who began to put aside his suspicions that Franz was a collaborator of ISIS under the supervision and control of Cal and knew more about the students' true mission than he was letting on.

Before leaving the hut, Franz told Buck, "Unlike my grandfather, I never blamed the German people for not supporting Hitler when the war turned sour. I blame Hitler's mother who told her son, 'Adolf, forget about being an artist. Throw your paint-by-the-numbers kit and your brushes and watercolors into the trash, get out of the house, and find yourself a job, and don't come back until you make something of yourself.'"

"She was prophetic, wasn't she?" asked Buck.

"Yes, she was pathetic too!" said Franz, nodding his head.

After Buck turned away from Franz to sneeze, Buck told him something he remembered about Mel Brooks. "Mel said during an interview many years ago, 'There is no way to get back at Hitler. My goal in life is to make the world laugh at Hitler. The only way to do it is by ridiculing him.'"

Franz paused to catch his breath then raised his voice a few decibels and admitted he had no reservation about invading the students' room because it was a perfect time since they were working in the fields. Furthermore, he confessed that there was no time to get a search warrant, and he was willing to take the risk and bear the consequences if his suspicions were wrong.

When Franz was near the end of his tirade, he confessed that his father sent him to America in 1939 to live with relatives in the German-speaking region of Lancaster, Pennsylvania.

"I was big and strong for a 10-year-old kid and quickly learned early in my stay everything there is to know about what it takes to be a successful farmer, thanks to the generosity of my Amish uncle," said Franz. "I returned to Germany after the war and bought this farm at Starnberger See in 1950 and dedicated my life to make it one of the finest in Bavaria. Even though I am 90 today and only half the man I was in my heyday, physically speaking, I still can give someone a good licking and take a licking as well and will never ever let anyone damage my reputation for excellence. It is imperative that my name never shall be mentioned, associated, or connected with ISIS."

"You look more like 65 than 90," said Buck who was impressed by his disclosure and complimented him.

"That's what comes from working 12 hours a day with animals and crops in the open air," answered Franz, "and drinking good Bavarian beer with weisswurst. But forgive me for digressing here. You're an American, and I am confiding in you because I trust you. I cannot imagine or accept the notion that you are associated with Cal. It doesn't add up or make sense. I am thoroughly confused."

Buck now thought about immediately reporting back to Chipmann the results of his visit but decided there was no time to lose in protecting Franz. Franz's life was at stake and Buck told him that he would make plans for his friend Marlene to care for him for a day or two.

Marlene was not expecting a phone call from Buck when she picked up the ringing phone, but she quickly sensed the desperation in his voice when he asked for her help.

"This is *Showtime!*" said Buck to Franz. "I want you to come with me to Fischbachau now because your life is in danger. You will have a caring mother and daughter to care for you until this crisis is resolved. Telephone your farm manager and tell him an emergency has forced you to leave everything in his hands and to call you if he has any questions or needs further instructions."

After Franz agreed to his wishes, Buck removed a necklace, kissed the Saint Christopher medal attached to it, and placed it around Franz's neck.

"It has always protected me," said Buck, "and now I want it to protect you."

"I think this is the beginning of a beautiful friendship," said Franz.

After leaving the hut, Buck and Franz paused about 10 feet from the door to catch a breath of fresh air. Suddenly, out of the field of sunflowers came a German Short-Haired Pointer flying straight toward them. Neither one moved from their side-by-side stance as the Pointer leapt onto Buck with a force that sent him tumbling backwards to the ground.

As the Pointer started licking Buck's face, Franz said, "I don't blame her for choosing a handsome young buck rather than an old farmer like me."

"I knew I had a way with women and occasionally tumbled head over heels," said Buck, "mostly due to seeing their two shapely legs instead of four on a Pointer."

Franz told Buck, "Her name is Moxie, a ten-year-old,

fourth-generation, female Pointer who is blessed with high intelligence and a good temperament. Her superior instinct in tracking is due to her incredible sense of smell."

"I surely don't smell at all like a rabbit," Buck said, "so it must have been something rabbity about my personality or behavior."

Then Franz explained that he put Moxie in her kennel before coming to meet Buck, but one of his employees probably heard her howling and let her out and she tracked him.

Ruby
A Pointer
Edmund Osthaus

"In other words, you are telling me that wherever you goest, she goest too!" Buck answered with a chuckle. "Well, we'll take Moxie with us to Fischbachau. This is no time to separate two friends."

Buck asked Franz to walk through the forest to the spot where he had parked his truck. Along the way Buck was in a playful mood and told him that Marlene was one of the best cooks in Bavaria.

"How old is Marlene?" asked Franz who managed for the first time to smile.

"Old enough to know better and keep out of trouble," answered Buck. "A woman never tells you her age—although she may lie about it."

After he made sure that Franz had his seatbelt secured with Moxie in his lap, Buck backed his pickup away from his hiding place onto the side road and headed in the direction of the main road to Fischbachau. He turned on an audio disc so that both could hear the popular recordings of Bert Klemperer and his orchestra. Klemperer's music seemed to alleviate Franz's nervousness as he reflected on the good times that he and his wife spent dancing to Klemperer's music.

Few words were spoken between them during the one-hour drive to Fischbachau. However, Buck thought to himself that this wonderful old farmer was someone he had known only for a few hours, and he liked what he saw. He said to himself that perhaps Franz could be part of his family and the grandfather that he never knew.

When Franz and Buck finally arrived at the Allesin's door, Franz was greeted by Erika who welcomed him to their home with a kiss on both cheeks. Afterward, Franz removed his shoes and left them beside the door. When he looked up, Marlene had her arms extended. Franz never hesitated to embrace her and told her that he never had such apprehensions about meeting someone, even on a blind date, and he had never felt more welcomed in his life.

In the meantime, while Franz and Buck were being welcomed by Marlene and Erika in Fischbachau, Cal drove his car up to the Funk farmhouse in Starnberger See and parked it close to the front door.

Cal took a minute to look over the field of sunflowers and

recognized Ali and Ben working on the engine of a farm thresher. Cal waved them over, and the three went into Franz's spacious farmhouse.

They gathered around a small table in the living room. When Ben could no longer hold back his anger he erupted in a tirade telling Cal how Franz had invaded their room and removed their secret papers. Ben cursed in Arabic at the beginning, middle, and end of each sentence.

Ali then expressed his displeasure for Franz's failure to teach them faster about growing top-quality crops and to stop reiterating obvious statements over and over. He told Cal that he and Ben had expected to make a small fortune later when they returned home and replicated the best hops to produce beer and capitalize on the growing potential of microbreweries in the Middle East.

At this precise moment Cal intended to put Ben and Ali at ease by putting his arms around their shoulders but both shrugged him away. Ben remained outraged and blamed Cal for not screening this farmer when contracts were made for the student exchange program.

"That is nonsense and a lie," said Cal. "All of the farmers selected were gullible and knew nothing about my association with ISIS. Furthermore, for your information, it did not take much effort to lure Max into our scheme to transmit data by inserting a microchip in the mane of his horses. All I had to do was hand him cash when he cried out, 'Show me the money!' But he developed a Napoleonic complex, turned into an ambitious renegade, and had to be eliminated."

"What you say may be true, but our cover is blown as well as yours," Ben told Cal, "and I do not see a way to fix it."

"Leave that to me," answered Cal, who asked what evidence they had to support their contention that Franz invaded and pilfered material from their room.

"We have been waiting impatiently since I telephoned you yesterday to show you what we found," Ben said as he and Ali led Cal to their room on the second floor.

They showed him the surveillance camera installed for security purposes and the video playback of Franz making a thorough search of the room and carefully removing some papers stored in the top drawer of Ben's desk. Franz evidently hoped that their removal would not be discovered immediately.

"You told me yesterday that these were secret documents," Cal said. "If they were so secret, why didn't you hide them in a secure place? On the surface it appears that you were negligent, and negligence is never acceptable or an excuse. Don't you agree?"

Cal's response only inflamed the outrage stirring in Ben's mind and the air in the room suddenly turned hotter than in a Swedish steam bath.

Cal then uttered somewhat of a death threat. "You may wish you were dead if news of your negligence and panic should reach higher authority in Saudi Arabia."

At this juncture, only a foot separated their noses when Ben faced Cal. Ben again could not control himself and began to chastise Cal for taking almost a day, a full day, to respond and to appear at their doorstep. Both were on the verge of a fistfight that could jeopardize the entire student exchange scheme in Bavaria.

Thankfully, Ali managed to separate them and settle things down. He explained that he and Ben had a grueling eight hours in the field, all because Franz ordered them to remove two stumps with a pick axe and break up ten large rocks with a sledgehammer. He contended that it was an assignment worse than anything that a convict on a chain gang would endure. After this assignment was completed, they were asked to check the engine of the thresher, which had a problem turning over. Ali ended his explanation by telling Cal that all of this hard labor contributed to Ben's outrage and current state of mind.

Cal wiped the sweat from his forehead and managed to explain that he had a full schedule with other farmers that had a higher priority, and he did not appreciate their outburst that showed no respect for authority. He made it clear there is no room for a panic when facing a crisis. He paused to take another look at the video that was looping and told them that in time each would gain intelligence, experience, and confidence to act under fire with a cooler head.

"All is not lost, my boys, because you have plenty of moxie," said Cal, pulling a switchblade from under his shirt for them to see. "When you've got moxie, you need hardware for protection."

"Fuck the moxie," Ben screamed to Cal. "Are you shitting me about the need for knives and guns when we need first to find a way out of this cesspool."

Ali stepped in and told Ben, "You better check your blood pressure. You are on the verge of losing your mind."

"Fuck my blood pressure," Ben shouted in a high-pitched voice. "We could be facing deportation tomorrow and dismissal by the Saudi Royal family and possible imprisonment."

Cal tried to make it clear that ISIS was not ready for another hijacking and their ambitious undertaking was too risky at this time. He then added that he would support them to his dying days but only on orders from the Middle East bosses.

Cal walked out of the room slowly and while descending the staircase, snapped his fingers and realized that Ben and Ali were desperate renegades. Because of their clash, it became clear that Ben and Ali must be removed in the same way Max was neutralized, with the use of a sedative.

About a minute later all three were reassembled in the living room where Cal took the initiative and asked them to join him in a toast to their new understanding, "Something to die for," spoken rhetorically, of course.

However, paradoxically, Cal underestimated the students who were not the least inclined to buy into his overture, especially when he told them that he would support them to his dying day.

A minute later, Cal went over to a small bar in the living room and asked them whether they preferred scotch or *boybin*, which was Cal's way of pronouncing bourbon.

Ben exclaimed, "No whiskey for me. This is wine country and best known for Riesling."

Ali said, "We prefer wine, please."

"So be it," said Cal and held up a bottle of Riesling reserve for their approval. At this point Cal was prepared to add a sedative to two of the glasses, but first needed to distract Ben and Ali by pointing to a painting over the fireplace.

"You have only about an hour to walk to the lake where you can swim in warm water and rent a sailboat like the one shown in the painting over the fireplace. I have admired it each time I pay a visit to Franz. It is an impressionist work by the Munich painter Otto Pippel."

Frühlings am Fang Starnberger See
Springtime Fishing at Starnberger Lake
Otto Pippel

However, Ben and Ali were not distracted by Cal's ploy and concentrated their eyes on the reflection in the mirror as they watched him add a powder, presumably a sedative, to the two end glasses in the row of three glasses.

After Cal brought the tray of drinks and placed it on a coffee table, Ali told him that it was time for a prayer and invited him to join them.

Ben, Ali, and Cal knelt and began to pray. When their prayers were completed, there was a burst of thunder and the living room lights flickered momentarily. Ben faked a dizzy spell and grabbed Cal's arm for support. It was long enough for Ali to switch one of the glasses from its end position to the middle.

Ben and Ali each picked up the two end glasses – Ben's end glass was the one Ali had switched; it did not contain the drug -- and waited for Cal to swallow his glass of wine. Cal savored the Riesling and was confident that he had administered the drug to them. Cal never noticed the switcharoo – or what hit him.

This time a burst of lightning struck close to the main house and caused another momentary flicker of the electricity in the house. There was silence for the next two to three minutes as both Cal and Ali were sedated.

Ben then carried Ali to a sofa and afterward managed to hoist Cal to his shoulder and carried him out of the farmhouse. To his surprise a light rain was falling and Cal's body kept slipping out of his grasp as he was gasping for air.

"You son of a bitch," Ben exclaimed because it took all of his strength to hoist Cal's slippery body onto the top of the thresher. "You must have lead up your ass."

Ben climbed into the driver's seat and squirmed a little because the seat had a slight puddle of rain water. When he tried to start the engine, it failed to turn over and instead kept repeating a cycle as if the carburetor were flooded. He grew more frustrated and cursed the engine in Arabic then pounded the dashboard.

Twenty seconds went by as if it were a lifetime before the

motor started with a roar that echoed across the field of drenched sunflowers. The roar of the motor almost lifted Ben out of his seat.

About a minute later, he slowed the engine to an idle then pushed and rolled Cal's body into the blades of the thresher. A few louder gasps were murmured by Cal as Ben took the steering wheel and turned the thresher in a wide circle three times. It was his intent that Cal's body was ground completely into fertilizer.

Ben lifted his head back to let the light rain wash his face then took a deep breath to smell the rainfall. He felt as if he now were cleansed of all pains and heard the sound of the rainfall in his ears. It was a moment of high anxiety in which only a murderer could hear raindrops.

Afterward Ben carried Ali up the stairs to their room. He had some difficulty turning the doorknob and once inside the hall light cast a shadow on Ali's bed. Ben gently lowered Ali's head onto a pillow to let him sleep off the effects of the sedative.

After taking a step, Ben accidentally stepped on the tail of Ali's cat that had fallen asleep under the bed.

"You fuckin' feminine feline!" Ben cursed in Arabic when the cat let out an incredibly loud scream. "Why don't you make yourself useful and find a rat to chew on?"

The following morning, with Cal's body ground into fertilizer, the only remains in the field still visible were the lenses of Cal's spectacles that were standing upright in the plowed circle. Each lens was the size of the bottom of a Coke bottle. It was remarkable, perhaps ironic, that the refraction of the lens in the morning sun produced a small rainbow across Franz's farm. It foretold what Confucius may have said about rainbows: "Every rainbow may look good from a distance but there is no guarantee a pot of gold is found at one end."

The next day around 10:30 a.m. everyone at Marlene and Erika's house was late to appear around the dining table because no one went to bed before midnight. After everyone had settled in the living room the night before, Marlene served an assortment of finger sandwiches and wine to welcome Franz to her family. Franz did not need any encouragement in telling them about his life and times as a farmer. It turned out that he was somewhat of a Hans Christian Anderson with an assortment of poignant experiences distilled from his 90 years on earth. There were no fairy tales although it seemed as if he milked a few incidents to get a laugh or two.

As they all sat down to the delicious brunch — which included homemade muffins topped with walnuts, stacks of buttermilk pancakes, and spicy sausage links from Nuremburg — Erika put one of her treasured Bert Klemperer recordings on the phonograph. Franz's eyes lit up with delight as he told Erika that they shared a love of Klemperer's music.

"I love his sense of rhythm," said Erika enthusiastically.

"And I love his exciting orchestrations!" Franz beamed.

Franz asked Buck to pass him the maple syrup for his pancakes and told Marlene that he slept like a baby and could not remember a better night without nightmares. He told everyone that living here for only a few hours seem to flush out all the misery that had filled his mind for the last month or so. He watched Buck who was sitting across from him at the round oak table as he used his fingers to dip one of the tasty links in ketchup and then licked his fingers.

"That is exactly how we did it when I was with my Amish family in Lancaster, Pennsylvania," said Franz. "Those *Tastylinks*, as we called them, seem to taste better when eaten without the benefit of a knife and fork."

In the middle of brunch, Buck's cell phone rang and he hesitated to answer it, especially with greasy fingers. But Erika encouraged him to take the call because it might be something important.

Chipmann was calling to bring Buck up to date.

"About an hour after sunup," said Chipmann, "Ben and Ali were arrested on the autobahn for driving a vehicle recklessly and for operating a vehicle without a driver's license and owner's registration."

"Where did they get a car?" asked Buck.

"They did not have to go far for wheels to make their escape because Cal parked his Porsche right outside the front door of Franz's house," Chipmann told him. "A policeman told me that Cal's car was souped up with an engine rated at 600 horsepower and able to go from zero to 60 miles an hour in four seconds."

"If the car was driven erratically," said Buck, "the driver must've thought he was Steve McQueen or Gene Hackman behind the wheel."

"Fortunately, three truck drivers were following the Porsche as it weaved in and out of three lanes until it suddenly slowed down probably because it ran out of gas. At this moment, the truckers were able to box it in and force it across the shoulder and into a field of soybeans. The truckers had everything recorded on their digital cameras and had phoned the police after spotting the erratic behavior of the driver behind the wheel of the Porsche."

"Did Ben and Ali put up a fight or resist their arrest?" asked Buck. "I would have suspected that they were armed with guns and ready for a shootout."

"Fortunately, Ben and Ali were not armed; they surrendered peacefully. They were separated from one another and handcuffed to the backseat of a police car and are now in a high security cell in the basement of the Justice Building in Munich awaiting interrogation by Schwartz."

Chipmann explained that during the one-hour drive from the soybean field to Munich, Ali wanted to come clean. So he confessed to an officer guarding him in the back seat of the police car that he and Ben realized Cal was a threat if he reported their behavior back to ISIS, and Cal had to be eliminated immediately.

"I guess by confessing now," said Buck, "Ali is no fool and realized it was better to go to prison in Germany than to go to prison in Saudi Arabia."

Chipmann told Buck that Ali explained how Cal's attempt to drug them was short-circuited because they managed to switch the glasses with the drug so that only one of them was sedated along with Cal. The next morning Ben told him that it was a struggle to carry Cal's body because it kept slipping from his grasp due to the rain and that he eventually pushed Cal's body into the thresher. Ben claimed it was justifiable homicide to do away with Cal because he intended to do away with them. Ben referred to it as a clear case of self defense.

"This is an incredible sequence of events too good to imagine happening, especially because it helps to remove any lingering suspicions about Franz collaborating with ISIS." said Buck. "I wish I could have been given the chance to photograph everything because no one would believe it later without some proof or hard evidence. Now, where does that leave us?"

"I am speaking to you from the living room inside Franz's farmhouse where we collected the two glasses with traces of the sedative. I would like you to drive Franz here as soon as possible," said Chipmann. "We still have to find Cal's last remains, but at least ISIS will be minus two of its soldiers posing as exchange students since their visas have been revoked. Furthermore, they soon will be indicted for the murder of Cal."

"Does that mean Franz is free to return to his farm?" asked Buck.

"In a nutshell, yes. I am convinced that it is safe for Franz to resume farming without any immediate threat of retaliation, but I would like to meet with him. Please drive him here as soon as possible so that I can have a short talk with him."

"Not so fast, Herr Chipmann. Please give Franz at least one more day here to recover his sanity and enjoy the hospitality so tenderly given to him by Marlene and Erika," Buck pleaded.

"Very well, provided you drive him here tomorrow and see that he is as comfortable as possible. I have to be in Munich and consult with Schwartz who will interrogate Ben and Ali and that will not be much fun for him or them, I assure you."

After Buck completed his conversation with Chipmann, Franz

lifted his head toward heaven and said, "There is some satisfaction that comes when you suspect the worst about someone and your suspicion is validated."

Everyone clapped and applauded Franz and told him he was the new hero of Fischbachau.

CHAPTER 8

In a high security section of the basement of the Justice Building, Ben and Ali were in individual cells awaiting interrogation by Schwartz. Ali occupied the cell nearest the entrance, and Ben was in a far cell so that they could not communicate with each other during their incarceration. A security guard was positioned outside each cell to monitor their conduct. Ali was pacing up and down nervously in his cell whereas Ben was very composed and sat motionless on his cot.

At precisely 9:30 AM, Schwartz's voice came over the loudspeaker with the order to bring Ali immediately to the interrogation room. Before he left his cell, Ali was handcuffed by his security guard who walked beside him until they faced a facial recognition monitor. The guard entered a security code and displayed his face which allowed them to enter the room. Once inside, Schwartz gave the guard permission to unlock Ali's handcuffs and ordered Ali to take a seat behind a table. At this point, Schwartz turned on the tape recorder.

Schwartz began his interrogation by reciting a lengthy listing of the charges against Ali, with the hope that he would answer questions about the possibility of Bavarian farmers who were involved in the student exchange program and who may have been witting or unwitting collaborators of ISIS. During this recitation, Ali bowed his head and listened to every word.

Ali was eager to speak and pledged to cooperate fully with Schwartz in revealing details of his experiences and intentions over the past two months on his assigned farm. He was especially eager to talk about two of the charges: first, the discovery of the maps and notes that were construed as a terrorist plot and second, the disappearance of Cal. He explained to Schwartz that he could not remember anything after having a glass of wine that must have contained a sedative. Ali emphasized that all he could remember the following morning after being drugged was a short conference with Ben who told him that he had taken care of Cal and that was all Ali needed to know. The less he knew, the better.

Schwartz began to perspire and was forced to remove his suit coat. He then walked over to the thermostat to adjust the temperature inside the interrogation room. He then brazenly removed the leather harness strap around his shoulder and waist with his service revolver inside its holster and leaned it against the wall at the far side of the table.

Schwartz's act was not a careless act like some gum-shoe, gum-chewing, lollypop-sucking detective. He was smart and clever enough to solve a problem when he faced it and brave enough to take responsibility into his own hands. In this case it was his intention to find out if Ali might be tempted to seize the gun and carry out an ISIS goal of killing as many important people as possible.

When Schwartz walked to a far corner for a drink of water from the dispenser, Ali snatched the holster and removed the gun. Schwartz told him the gun was loaded and all he had to do was squeeze the trigger and ascend to heaven for killing a high federal officer of the German government.

For the first time, a smile crossed Ali's face as he took a moment to study the gun and move his fingers across the barrel and stock. But he promptly replaced it in its holster and told Schwartz, "I have been a witness to enough killing in my lifetime. I have been indoctrinated and radicalized in Iran by ISIS teachers, but I must turn away from such conduct and hopefully you, Officer Schwartz, will show some leniency here."

Schwartz thanked Ali and told him, "You made the right decision that saved your life. Your destiny will now be in the hands of the prosecutor. I guarantee that you will be given a fair trial for being an accessory in the disappearance of Cal. Your actions and answers here this morning surely will not hurt you."

"That's a relief, believe me," answered Ali who then told him about an oncoming migraine headache and dizziness that was becoming unbearable. He asked for some medication and to be excused from further questioning.

Schwarz felt sympathetic and told Ali that he often suffered the same thing from stress and keeps a supply of pills with him wherever he goes.

Ali asked him point blank for the name of the pills.

"Meclizine," answered Schwartz who walked over to his suit coat, removed a pill from a pill box and handed it to him. "I have been thinking recently about going into another business that has less stress and pays as well with the same challenge and happiness."

"I hope and pray that someday I will get a chance to go into another business too," Ali replied.

<hr />

After Ali returned to his cell, Ben was escorted to the interrogation room. When the guard, Sergeant Ellsworth Doppo, removed Ben's handcuffs he accidentally pinched Ben's wrist causing Ben to let out a scream and to jab his fist into the guard's ribs.

"You pig, you pinched me with those handcuffs intentionally, didn't you?" Ben screamed.

"I'll show you what pain is, you bastard," said Doppo as he grabbed Ben's arms and lifted him a few inches off the floor and pushed his head against the concrete wall.

Schwartz reacted immediately by separating the guard from Ben and bellowed out, "For Christ's sake, get control of yourself, man. You don't want to lose your pension over this lowlife."

Doppo wiped some sweat from his face and apologized for losing control. Schwartz interrupted him and told him there was no need to apologize to someone whose mission it was to kill innocent people. He told Doppo to take his post outside the room and whispered into his ear that his outburst may be the catalyst needed to pry open Ben's conscience and finally get the information they had been seeking.

"It's time to seize the day... ...Carpe Diem," Schwartz uttered.

Ben was relieved after he watched his guard leave the interrogation room and began to examine the wall around him more carefully. He suspected, and rightly so, that there was a two-way mirror on the corridor side.

Schwartz started the questioning by reciting again the charges against him, which were a repetition of those leveled against Ali. At the conclusion, he asked Ben if he would like a cup of coffee.

"I like Yemeni coffee and Italian espresso," Ben answered. "It's strong, just like me."

"Did you ever taste a better coffee than these two?" Schwartz asked in a louder voice.

"I don't remember," uttered Ben.

"Do you remember preparing notes and schematics and maps that might be construed as a plan for terrorist acts?"

"I don't remember."

"Do you remember how and where Cal disappeared?"

"No, I don't remember."

"Here we go again with your favorite expression and answer," said Schwartz. "Sooner or later, you are going to admit something to show that my time here was not wasted."

"Plow ahead," answered Ben. "Maybe if you dig deeper, you might find a nugget."

"We show in our records that you spent six months in Iran. A tourist, I presume."

"You can call it that and anything else you want to, but my answer is still the same. I don't remember."

"Do you know what it is to be radicalized?"

"If I answer 'yes,' are you going to force me to explain it? Otherwise, my answer is 'no.'"

Schwartz walked over to a small table near the door and removed a porcelain cup from a supply next to the coffee dispenser. He slammed the cup down so forcefully in front of Ben that it sounded like a gun shot and reverberated around the concrete block walls. Ben remained frozen in his seat and showed no emotion whatsoever until he noticed how exasperated Schwartz had become.

"Out with it," screamed Schwartz. "Admit that you were the assassin who took care of Cal. Confession is good for the soul. Revealing the truth and how you did away with Cal will make you stronger and you will feel closer to Allah."

"Where's my coffee?" Ben asked, staring into the empty cup. He turned it slowly around then upside down. "I don't see any fuckin' coffee!"

"It's brewing," Schwartz answered now in a slower, more deliberate voice, "just like you."

"Are you now going to read me my rights to have a lawyer present and tell me that anything said by me may be taken down and used as evidence against me in a trial?"

"I read you those rights yesterday. Don't you remember?"

"I can't remember even what I had for breakfast this morning or if I even had breakfast in jail. Speaking of jail, I never slept a wink last night. I need some rest, and I need it now before I collapse."

"You'll have plenty of rest, I assure you, by the time this session is over provided you cooperate and tell me how, when, and where you were recruited by ISIS and how you were trained and deployed as an ISIS exchange student assigned to a Bavarian farmer."

"My memory and mind are a blank," Ben answered and squirmed in his chair. "I would like to cooperate but cannot remember anything. I told you over and over my memory is a blank. Why are you constantly repeating your questions? By the way, where is my coffee that you offered me five minutes ago."

"How is it that you can remember my offer so precisely? I told you it's brewing."

Ben said that he could not smell or see anything being brewed in the coffee dispenser and began to squirm in his chair.

"Oh, it's there, believe me," answered Schwartz. "It's a special blend where the beans must be ground into a very fine powder, all invisible to the naked eye but visible with infra-red goggles."

"I think you are bullshitting me, Officer Schwartz," Ben said in a louder tone.

Schwartz pretended to ignore Ben's comments and said, "Earlier when I asked you where you were on October 10th, four days ago, you told me that you did not remember and you even could not remember what you had for breakfast that morning."

"Why don't you let me rest for an hour or more?"

"For the same reason you didn't let Cal, one of your ISIS colleagues, rest for an hour or so before you killed him."

"No quid pro quo for helping you in your pursuit of ISIS, Counselor. I can tell you nothing about ISIS because I never even heard of the terrorist band. I have nothing to give or trade for information. Next question."

"Let's get down to specifics. When I asked you if you were at the Oktoberfest during its run in Munich, did you say that you had no recollection?"

"If that's what I said, that's what I said. I wasn't lying or trying to be evasive. By the way, aren't you supposed to read me my rights to have a lawyer present?"

"I told you just a few minutes ago that you were read your rights when you were arrested yesterday. Have you forgotten it already?"

"O.K. You're right. Now why don't you stick your head up your ass."

"I suggest you remember that vulgarity is taken into account when sentencing is considered by the court."

Schwartz smiled and grew stronger at being able finally to rattle Ben enough so that he might reveal something about the dynamics of ISIS, its strategy, and its way of enlisting and deploying recruits.

"If you have no objections, what would you say if I now played a video of you and Ali at the Oktoberfest?"

"You can do whatever you want to do but that was not me inside the Paulaner Brewery hangar!" exclaimed Ben.

"How is it that you remember precisely the name of the brewery sponsoring the hangar but cannot recall being there?"

"I take that back what I said about being inside that hangar. It just slipped out due to stress and anxiety."

Now Schwartz lost his composure and shouted, "You may sing like a lark, but you are still a rat — and once a rat, always a rat. I would offer you a shot of whiskey to relax your nerves, but you are quite relaxed enough."

At this point Schwartz surmised that his ability and methods to antagonize Ben were working and decided to cut to the chase.

Schwartz asked Ben, "You said you were in your room sleeping off the drug Cal put into your glass of wine, but you said you watched through a window as Ali carried Cal's body to the thresher and lifted him onto the cab. Do you remember making that statement yesterday?"

"If you have it recorded, then that is the way it went down."

"It is hard if not impossible to imagine that Ali, who weighs about 140 pounds, can carry Cal's body from the farmhouse into the meadow and lift Cal's 180 pounds, dead weight, onto the thresher."

"Huh?"

"You also said that you watched through that same window in your room as Ali dropped Cal's body into the thresher then drove it in a circle three times, right?"

"Ah, that's right."

"You are not a good liar, Ben. There is only one window in your room and it faces the back of the farmhouse. Furthermore, if you were drugged with rohypnol like Cal was, there is no way in hell that you could see anything clearly visible beyond 10 feet. I doubt if the court will be lenient when your testimony is given with these contradictions, inconsistencies, and lies."

Schwartz paused to wipe the sweat from his brow. "Furthermore, Ben, when you are sent back to Saudi Arabia they will not hold a parade for you or give you a medal. You know they won't put you on a Wheaties box; they will string you up by your balls!"

"I have nothing further to add here. I need some rest," Ben told Schwartz, as he breathed and perspired heavily. "Where's my coffee? A cup right now would give me strength to go on with your questioning."

"How is it you can remember a cup of coffee coming up and can't remember details about killing Cal?"

"I've told you over and over that I have a problem remembering things."

"How long have you had this problem?"

"What problem?" Ben asked with a face of stone.

At this point, Schwartz repeated exactly the same steps he had taken when interrogating Ali Shiptoshur, starting with removing his shoulder harness and gun and walking over to the water dispenser.

As Schwartz swallowed a cup of chilled water, Ben Ladeen reached for Schwartz's holster, removed the gun, and played with it a minute or two. Ben then waved Schwartz over and ordered him to take a seat.

"The tides of war have turned in my favor, you bastard," Ben shouted. "Now, it is my time to interrogate you."

"For better or worse?" asked Schwartz. "No quid from you, but you expect quo from me?"

"I don't have a fuckin' clue what you're talking about. I have nothing to hide, trade, or lose at this point," Ben scoffed.

"Only your life," answered Schwartz. "You can never escape this facility. A gunshot will lock down the entire building. There is no escape because you don't know the keypad numbers to open the door. Is killing me worth the court sentencing you to death for killing a government official? Is taking my life now equivalent to giving up your life later? If it is, squeeze the trigger and begin your ascent to Allah."

Ben's face twisted into a devilish smile and he slowly panned the gun as if on a dolly to Schwartz's forehead.

"Think twice, *Slick*," said Schwartz. "That gun has a hair trigger. Don't squeeze it until you are absolutely sure of your intent. Will ISIS give you a citation and medal for killing me that is equivalent to their blowing up a bus loaded with school children?"

Ben stood up and pointed the gun at Schwartz's forehead. He pulled the trigger, but the gun failed to fire. He pulled the trigger several times to no avail. He pointed the gun at his temple and again it failed to fire.

Schwartz rose calmly and walked over to the water cooler and swallowed a second full cup. To prevent anyone from watching the interrogation through a two-way mirror, he turned off the lights inside the room, then donned night vision goggles he had hidden in his back pocket. He removed his personal gun—not his service revolver—that was hidden under his shirttails and calmly walked back to confront Ben again.

Ben could not see Schwartz standing before him but heard his footsteps as he asked, "Have you ever heard of Ali Sonboly?"

"Nein," Ben answered in German as he dropped the gun on the table.

"My sister was in a McDonald's in Munich on July 22nd, 2016. She placed an order for a Big Mac, but all she got was a whopper from Sonboly when he shot her in the back and killed eight others and wounded 35. Did I mention that he was radicalized in Iran in one of the terrorist cells under ISIS control? Maybe you were radicalized in Iran, too, and loved it."

Schwartz's eyes began to water and clouded his eyesight momentarily. He imagined how the last moments of his sister's life may have unfolded inside McDonald's.

"Sonboly was a soldier like you, working for ISIS, with a plan to kill as many innocent people as possible in as short a time as possible," Schwartz said. "What Ali Sonboly has done can never be undone, but his rampage will look good on his resume when he faces Allah, just like your plan to hijack a plane will."

"How long are you going to keep me in the dark," Ben asked him.

"Be patient, Ben," Schwartz answered. "You will soon get all the rest you need, enough for a lifetime on this planet, enough for eternity and beyond."

"Bullshit," Ben answered. "You're shitting me, aren't you? How can time be extended beyond eternity?"

"That's artistic license, Ben. Call it what you will, but I am not being deceitful or lying. Truth is on the march and so is justice," said Schwartz. "Do you remember what a prominent person, perhaps Confucius, said a long time ago?"

"This is no time for a quiz or lecture, Professor, or propaganda about democracy."

"The saying is that the victim leaves his ghost like a shadow to trail the murderer until the murderer is dead."

"Fuck who ever said that, and you can put that in your notes, too," said Ben. "You always thought I was indecisive. Now I am not so sure."

"Let me make myself perfectly clear or even clearer," Schwartz answered. "Permit me to try a different tack in my questioning. There is no one in your life now—except me. No one who cares about you or who will save you. Why don't you sign over your life insurance to me as sole beneficiary? I will make sure you have a good send off to Allah."

"Have you lost your mind?" asked Ben. "You would be the last person I would trust to spend my money wisely. For Allah's sake, you are wearing me down, physically and mentally. How many times do I have to ask you for some rest?"

"Just a wee bit longer, long enough to ask a favor. If and when you see Allah, tell him enough is enough and more than enough. The brutality and killing must end sooner rather than later."

"Your words are killing me."

"You haven't heard or seen anything yet. The best is yet to come after you answer one last question." Schwartz paused and took a deep breath. His muscles expanded. "Do you pick your toes?"

"Huh? You must be joking…or groping."

"I am serious, believe me. Do you pick your toes?"

Ben gasped for a breath of air but only swallowed a stinky sour mouthful. He was completely nonplussed by Schwartz's question. He did not get Schwartz's reference to "The French Connection."

"Why don't you fuck off, Inspector," Ben muttered.

"I'll take that as a 'yes,'" answered Schwartz, who then remembered to check that Ben had not concealed a fork or knife somewhere on his legs. Schwartz adjusted his night vision goggles and stared at Ben's ankle and gradually looked up from his ankle to his knees to his groin.

At this point Schwartz remarked, "Before, I thought you were crazy, but now I see your nuts."

Ben sighed loudly and drew enough strength to ask Schwartz one final question, one that seemed to come out of the blue.

"What would it take to let me go?"

"Let you go?" responded Schwartz instantaneously. "Where would you like to go?"

"For starters, anywhere out of your sight."

"We are way past *Let's Make a Deal*. Your life is much more complicated."

Schwartz took a deep breath for a moment while his full strength returned. He now believed that Ben was ready to unburden his conscience, which was a warehouse of secrets.

Suddenly Ben's face became dark and shrouded.

"You are right," he told Schwartz. "My life is too complicated for one of your simple-ass deals. I'm finished. There is no more to say."

"Your resistance amazes me, Ben," said Schwartz, "so much so that I am forced to use profanity and tell you it's almost time for you to fuck off!"

Schwartz was so pissed off that he spit at Ben's forehead. It was an action worthy of Clint Eastwood.

"Now look what you have done to make me this mad, Ben. Now I'll have to take time off to attend a course in Anger Management."

Schwartz then moved his gun inches away from the phlegm on Ben's forehead and asked, "Would you like to sail away on the Queen Mary if it can be arranged in exchange for telling me what led you to become an ISIS exchange student? I am perplexed that you accepted such a low position in the ISIS hierarchy when you have demonstrated that you are a man of higher intelligence and intellect."

"Fuck off, you cocksucker. Up to now, I thought you were such an intelligent detective. Everyone knows that Queen Mary can no longer sail. She is a tourist attraction in America. I guess you were trying to trap me, weren't you?"

"Trap, you say," said Schwartz, "like you trapped Cal by switching drinks? The next sound you hear will be a shot from the muzzle of my gun, a speeding bullet right between your eyes."

When the tension was at its highest, Ben surprised Schwartz by repeating in the loudest voice that he could muster, "What would it take to let me go free?"

"Take to go free?" Schwartz asked with a satanic grunt and grin.

"At this point, you could offer me the moon and all the stars in the sky and even reincarnation of my sister but the die is cast, you bastard. Your indifference for the rights of humanity has done you in at last. Even if you were to undergo a metamorphosis, your past is a prologue that can never be changed. It is time for you to join Allah.

"I can safely tell you that you are completely insensitive to inflicting suffering, indifferent to joy, and therefore you are about to meet your destiny. From the start of my interrogation my objective was to get a statement of your complicity in the murder of Cal, which …"

"You have not a chance in hell of getting such a statement," Ben interrupted him. "You can go …"

This time Schwartz interrupted Ben by pounding his fist on the table top then looked closer at Ben's face that was now frozen. Ben's mouth was open wide as if he were trying to cry out in frustration but couldn't. His eyes bugged out as wide as humanly possible without a single blink. It was as if Ben's entire body was stiff and ready for a coffin.

Schwartz's index finger began to squeeze the trigger.

It seemed like a lifetime, but finally a single gunshot was heard and echoed around the room. It resounded as if it were from a repeating rifle.

As Ben's bloody head landed on the table, Schwartz said, "Never underestimate the power of *The Schwartz*." He then replaced the empty cartridge of the gun that was in Ben's hand with a fully-loaded cartridge and turned the lights back on.

Schwartz noticed that there was not as much blood coming from Ben's forehead as might be expected. He said to himself, "Perhaps ISIS recruits don't shed their blood. They make others shed theirs. I'll say one thing about this bastard. He was defiant to the end and remained committed to ISIS."

The following day, when Schwartz was interviewed by agents in Internal Affairs, he submitted a written declaration that Ben Ladeen was not killed or murdered by him but executed in the line of duty and in self-defense. He then declared that he was submitting his resignation from the force because of increasing duress and unfathomable stress. He said that it was an inevitable and sad ending to a 25-year career with the Bureau.

As he was leaving the Internal Affairs interrogation, Schwartz noticed one of the agents who had been especially quiet and only took notes but asked no questions.

"I'm going to *Disneyworld!*" Schwartz smiled and bellowed at the top of his voice. He quickly pulled the agent closer to him and whispered, "That is provided there is as much money in my retirement account as I think there is. Confidentially, Marlene

Allesin doesn't know it yet, but I am going to propose to her—that I help her run her new business. With her permission, I would like to be a partner in her truffle business. Remember: It's good to be the Truffle King!"

CHAPTER 9

Around noon, a friendly neighbor farmer, Herman Hillstoup, knocked at Marlene's door. Hillstoup was a 45-year-old, handsome widower who resembled the actor Horst Buckholz. He had his eye on Marlene even before he was married, but he was afraid to make any advances because Marlene was married to Max. Herman's wife died a year ago; he now had an opportunity to express his feelings and to help Marlene recover from the recent loss of her husband.

Hillstoup apologized for his impromptu visit and explained that he had seen much activity over the past few days and asked what was going on and if everything was in order.

Marlene invited him to have a cup of coffee and a piece of cake from the Winkelstüberl Inn bakery. She remembered that Max felt Herman was a good neighbor, one of the few Max could trust.

Herman told them that he often received a call from Max about problems Max encountered with his breeding of Trakehners. Herman also acknowledged that, for the past 15 years, he had been cross-breeding Aberdeen Angus cows with different native German cattle breeds, especially Gelbvieh, to produce bigger and heavier German Angus, known for their easy calving and good nature.

Herman stressed that Max was keen to apply Herman's breeding know-how to crossbreeding Trakehners with Arabian mares.

Herman told them that he was only invited once to set foot inside of Max's laboratory and that was after signing a statement of security never to reveal anything that he witnessed there. "Max was paranoid about anyone spying on him and stealing his technology, I guess," said Herman, smiling. "That's why he had so many mirrors scattered around his property; mirrors like the ones on the side of cars. More important, he was not of a take-and-give-back mentality. I don't remember him ever saying 'thank you' for answers to his questions about crossbreeding or solutions to any of his problems."

Although Marlene was somewhat reluctant at first to let Herman join her, Erika, and Buck as they went through Max's lab, when they had finished their coffee and cake, Marlene took a deep breath and asked Herman to join them in Max's lab to help unravel Max's connection to the Saudi Royal family.

After 30 minutes of moving books and apparatus around inside the lab, Schatze spotted a rat moving cautiously along one wall of the salt mine. Schatze followed the rat to the right end of the mine until it disappeared in a crevice. Buck realized that this area resembled a doorway probably bricked in around the closing months of World War II.

Buck noticed that the doorway resembled one in the film "The Monuments Men," which was about a small group of courageous American soldiers who searched in German salt mines to recover and identify works of art stolen by the Nazis during the closing years of World War II.

Buck remembered his father telling him about the time when Hitler's henchmen started to plunder Europe for art. His father said that the artworks were destined for installation in the Führer Museum in Austria.

Faced with a salt mine dilemma straight out of "The Monuments Men," and remembering his father's words, Buck told Marlene that explosives probably would be necessary and asked her to inquire what the government policy would be from this moment forward.

Within a minute or two, Marlene had telephoned the only person she knew in the Bavarian government, and that was Felix Chipmann who was head of the Homicide Bureau. He was a good first choice to get advice from because of the connections he formed during his years of service. If anybody would know how to proceed, he would.

When Chipmann received Marlene's telephone call, he realized the level of her anxiety. He had explained to her that the salt mine was a government-owned facility and the lab that Max constructed was illegal. He told Marlene that Hitler's Reichstag had requisitioned all the salt mines during World War II. Chipmann was intrigued and excited at the prospect of examining the mine and of finding more information about Cal and Max's relationship to the Saudi Royal family and to ISIS.

Chipmann ended their conversation by ordering Marlene not to proceed further until he could get some guidance and advice from the Bureau of Legal Affairs. He then took a deep breath and said, "Now would be a good time to cut through the proverbial red tape of government bureaucracy and play politics with friends in high places."

Three hours later Chipmann had returned to his office and was holding in his hands and kissing an officially-approved permit to use whatever means available to gain entry through the sealed doorway to the adjoining salt mine.

Chipmann realized at this point that he was taking on responsibilities outside his discipline; he felt understaffed. However, he had an ace in the hole and that was his former assistant, the recently retired Ernst Rolf Schwartz, a brilliant forensic detective. Chipmann thought it would be easy to entice Schwartz into joining him in this effort. It was easy—after he promised health benefits and an increase in Schwartz's former salary.

After Schwartz resettled in his old office, he and his boss conceived a plan of action for demolition of the salt mine wall between Max's lab and an unknown area of the mine. Schwartz was especially pleased to know he would be associated with Marlene because he was close to proposing a business arrangement with her in which he would manage her truffle business.

It took one week of intense work by government demolition experts before the doorway was finally opened.

The explosion after the detonation was followed by the sound of thousands of wings flapping. The door to the salt mine may have been sealed for entry by humans, but bats had found a way to enter and exit without being seen.

After the debris was cleared away, no one was allowed to enter this new section of the salt mine for fear of a booby trap such as a land mine. Specialists with sensors and metal detectors scanned the area and issued an All-Clear, deeming it safe to enter. Everyone moved cautiously into the storage area of the salt mine.

Eventually, Chipmann and Schwartz entered with their high-powered flashlights and noticed a single chest in a dark corner. From his university studies Chipmann recognized the chest as a wrought iron medieval German money chest.

Schwartz lagged behind because he was heavier and his shoes sank deeper into the bat guano that covered the floor of the mine. He yelled out to Chipmann, "I may not know bear spat when I see it, but I know pay dirt when I see it; and this is a gold mine of bat guano. Bats love an exceptionally dry climate, and this salt mine is a perfect home for them. Farmers will pay dearly for the nutrients of potassium, nitrogen, and phosphorus that the bat guano contains and that they can use to enrich the soil for their crops. The level of phosphorus in bat guano is particularly ideal for growing hops."

Schwartz's words failed to draw a response from Chipmann because Chipmann had bigger things to deal with.

Chipmann called in specialists in explosives and a locksmith to assess the safety of opening the money chest. The mine was cleared of all personnel, except for those who wore protective shielding in case the money chest was booby-trapped.

Two hours later, the chest was unlocked by the locksmith who told Felix that the lock mechanism was intricately welded to the dome and controlled by at least 18 bolts. Thankfully everyone was relieved to hear the news that the locksmith found no explosive devices in the locking mechanism.

Felix looked inside the chest and removed one of six parcels carefully protected by sawdust. He immediately recognized the velvet cover that bore the double eagle insignia of the Imperial House of Romanoff. He quickly returned the parcel to the chest and posted a guard with instructions to shoot to kill if anyone entered the cave. "No one, and I repeat no one, is permitted to enter, period!" he ordered.

In the ensuing minutes Felix was busy talking on his cell phone with the noted expert, Dr. Mai I. Kopafeel at the Dresden Museum's Grünes Gewölbe (Green Vault), a depository that held the most precious historical artifacts in Germany. Dr. Kopafeel, who was the director responsible for the museum's precious Russian arts such as Fabergé eggs, agreed to fly the next morning to Munich and be chauffeured to Fischbachau.

To say that she caused a sensation when she arrived was an understatement. The moment that she stepped out of the car, it was as though Botticelli's Venus arose from the halfshell. She was a vision to behold with a figure whose dimensions measured 38-24-36. This Aphrodite-like blond bombshell caused an earthquake inside the bodies of men trying their best to *not* stand at attention while standing at attention.

Felix did his utmost to whisk her as fast as possible into the salt mine so she could examine the contents of the chest. After she put on a protective apron and gloves, and a headlamp with magnification lenses, she began to unwrap each parcel. Her heartbeat became erratic as she began murmuring. Surprisingly, her hands were as steady as the Rock of Gibraltar. She dictated into the recorder attached to a lavaliere around her neck while photographing her findings with her high-resolution digital camera.

Two hours later she was introduced to Marlene, Erika, and Buck who were assembled inside the Allesin farmhouse for a presentation of her findings.

"I could spend several weeks explaining each of these precious objects to you and still feel I did not do justice to Fabergé's important work. A good way to begin is to tell you that Fabergé was noted first for his unique designs and second for the remarkable skill of admitting only the most accomplished master goldsmiths into his workshop. Within five years his firm invented more than 140 shades of different colors that he applied to his enamel work. It should be noted that secrecy was paramount in his workshop. Even the master who polished each work never revealed the secrets of his trade.

"A workman once was brought to tears when his creation, one that took more than a year to complete, was smashed to bits right before his eyes by Carl Fabergé. You may find this shocking but think about that poor worker who was brutally made aware of the high standards of the works that bore the name of Carl Fabergé!"

She then showed a photo that was slightly out of focus. It was one she had taken of herself after unfolding the first parcel. "Forgive me if it seems vain of me but I wanted the world to know what it was like to unearth a treasure-trove of art that had been buried for more than 70 years. My fingers were shaking but only for this first photograph."

The photographs Dr. Kopafeel had taken were each projected onto the screen to show a closeup of each Fabergé egg opened to show the surprise inside. More photos showed details of the designs and the ingenuity required to showcase the precious jewels, glittering enameling, and shimmering shades of color that changed depending on the direction of the light.

Everyone was in awe when she explained the importance and

the contributions of Fabergé's designers and the workmasters who fabricated the eggs.

"Because time is of the essence, I will hand my baton to Inspector Chipmann, but will take one or two questions," Dr. Kopafeel told them, slightly exhausted by the tense work she had performed.

Buck told her that he read about Fabergé at Lehigh and saw a Fabergé egg at the Walters Art Museum in Baltimore. "How do these eggs compare to those collected by such dignitaries as Henry Walters, Malcolm Forbes, and Marjorie Merriweather Post?"

"Equal if not superior," Dr. Kopafeel answered. "That is all I can tell you now."

With growing curiosity, Marlene asked, "I hope you will forgive the pun, but assuming you are a good egg and speak off the record, can you tell me about the value of these eggs?"

"Keep in mind that I am not an appraiser nor is anyone on the museum staff permitted to suggest a monetary value on any works of art. But I will speak off the record and not mince my words here. If these eggs were put up for sale at a major auction house, and two Russian oligarchs entered into a bidding war, I would expect each egg could fetch at least 10 million euros."

That statement caught everyone's attention and caused Marlene to go pale and almost slip from her chair. Erika rushed to hand her a bottle of water. Buck grabbed an apron and began fanning her with it.

When Marlene had somewhat recovered, she managed to tell them, "To think I was living beside such a treasure for all these years is truly mind boggling. I could have filled my bureau with dirndls from the best designers and supported a riding for the handicapped program."

As Marlene continued images passed through her mind of one of the happiest times of her life, "When I was in college I volunteered at a handicapped riding center. It was one of the most valuable experiences of my life. Ever since then I have wanted to start a similar center that would be a member of the Federation for Riding for the

Disabled International. Everyone gains from this type of program – the riders, the volunteers, and even the horses! I never thought I would have the means to do this, but now I have the desire *and* the means."

"I would have traveled the world in my own jet, just like Donald Trump," laughed Buck.

"Yumpin' yiminy," said Erika. "I could have bought the rights to lots of music from the '30s and '40s, and I could have covered myself with Hermés silk scarves."

About an hour later, Inspector Chipmann told Marlene that the money chest and its contents were government property and authorities were *en route* to take possession of them.

"Be prepared to sign a receipt for transfer of the money chest and its contents, and don't be surprised if they are offered first to the Russian government in exchange for the return of the art confiscated by the Russians when they conquered half of Germany during the final years of World War II. That art was confiscated from museums, collectors, and galleries and transported to Russia. It was considered collateral and mainly seized from East Germany and from countries such as the Netherlands, France, and Belgium."

The Inspector confided to Marlene that she may be entitled to a reward of perhaps as much as ten percent of the market value of the eggs.

"That's wonderful," said Marlene enthusiastically. "But don't forget that while you have the right to confiscate the medieval chest with the Faberge eggs, the bats inside the salt mine are on my farm – and their poop is mine, all mine!"

"Perhaps now is the time for a story with photos," said Buck, turning to Marlene and Erika for confirmation as he tried not to guffaw at Marlene's infatuation with bat guano.

"Let's think it over and be cautious here," said Marlene pointedly to Buck. "We do not want to rush into things without contemplating the benefits and consequences. Do you really want to open up a can of worms and tell the world about Max and his pimples and warts?

Do you want thousands of people, treasure hunters, scouring over Fischbachau in an Easter egg hunt for Fabergé eggs?"

Recognizing that Marlene was distressed, Herman took her arm and escorted her out of the lab. Then they strolled across the meadow leisurely with lots of questions popping into their minds. A minute later Marlene had regained her composure and started a conversation by asking Herman if he had any children.

He told her that he had two handsome twin sons, who were now 27 years old. He stopped and showed her a photo he took from his leather wallet. "One is named Ebenezer and the older one by an hour is Florenz. I call them Ebb and Flo. They are my best assets and are gifted chefs. Only God knows how, when, why, or where they got their gift for creating masterpieces with Danish Cherry Heering liqueur. In school they were known as the *Kirsche Kings*. Their specialties now are a ravishing plate of raebraten, similar to sauerbraten but with wild deer instead of beef, and forellen, fresh trout grown from their river hatchery."

Marlene's instantaneous reaction came as no surprise. "My God, one resembles Tyrone Power and the other, Maximilian Schell. Better not let Erika see the photo. Otherwise, Buck may be out in the cold!"

"They just graduated from the Kochschule Berlin—the best culinary arts academy in Germany," Herman said proudly. "They want to see the world before settling down and opening their own business. One thing is certain. They have no intention of living permanently in Germany. They have their sights on America, the land of opportunity. You need not fear that they would be drawn into a battle for Erika's love. They are intent on marrying twin girls, another somewhat wild and crazy notion."

Meanwhile, as Herman was conversing with Marlene, Buck had a hankering to mosey up to Dr. Kopafeel like a Trakehner foal looking for its dam. "I cannot begin to express my appreciation for your splendid work," he told her and asked for permission to show her a row of Tannenbaums that lined the meadow. "Please, may I offer you a seat on this park bench? I have been waiting patiently to ask if there is anything I can do to repay you."

She motioned him to take a seat first, but then hesitated to sit beside him. An impulse of caution flashed across her mind about his overture and possible intention. She felt exhausted by the work she had completed and was close to a decision about not flying back to Dresden that night. But she was not about to tell Buck or get his advice about where to spend the night. Something inside her sent up a red flare.

Buck tried to put her at ease by telling her, "I promise to keep both of my hands firmly attached to my wrists."

"But you haven't promised where your wrists are headed," she answered with renewed strength.

At this precise moment her interaction with Buck was interrupted by a telephone call from the Director of the Dresden Museum who informed Dr. Kopafeel that a limo was on its way with two security men to drive her and the chest immediately to the Flughafen Munchen, the modern Franz Josef Strauss Airport. He told her a private jet was ready to return her with the chest of Fabergé eggs to the Green Vault.

The phone conversation concluded with an order to keep everything a secret to avoid a possible attempt to hijack the chest. During the entire call Dr. Kopafeel uttered few words except "ja, ja, ja" and nodded in response to the Director's words while staring at Buck the entire time.

Obviously, Buck was getting the wrong signals as his spirits began to rise. He expected her to walk a few steps and take a seat next to him. He suddenly needed a moment to collect his thoughts so he closed his eyes, sighed, and leaned his head backward as far as it would go.

"You had a long and arduous day," he said to her in a sort of dream of imagination. "Where were you planning to sleep tonight? Would you like me to make a reservation at Winkelstüberl?"

"I have a responsibility that is taking me away from here. Unfortunately, I cannot disclose it to you," said Dr. Kopafeel.

At this moment her appearance went in and out of focus and Buck ignored her words that sounded muddled to him. He obviously was in his own world and feeling high and flighty. He had never seen such a combination of beauty, physically and mentally, in his lifetime. He was full of himself and feeling his oats, despite being very attracted to Erika. He brashly asked, "Would you like to see…" then paused to extend his camera strapped to his neck, "my Canon?" He was now gazing down at his groin.

In a flash Buck's imagination zoomed to higher heights as he now saw a vision of Dr. Kopafeel dressed in a sea-green see-through clingy negligee. She had been transformed from Aphrodite to *Aphronighty*. The vision drew closer and closer, moving in slow motion before his eyes. She spoke softly, "I must confess, Buck, that after two failed marriages, I am no longer so keen on men. In both instances, I thought my husband, under whom I worked so hard, was coming, not going!"

Now Buck's imagination took a higher leap and he began to feel giddy and carefree and decided to shoot the works with a double entendre. "Would you hold it against me if I told you that you have the most voluptuous body I've ever seen? Are you real or just a figment of my imagination?"

"Pass me your hand," the vision responded, "and I'll let you judge if I am real or not." She then let the top portion of her negligee fall off her shoulders.

Steam started to rise out of Buck's ears as he heard a voice echoing from somewhere behind the Tannenbaums. It was the voice of doom that told him, "Be careful, Buck. You may be biting off more than you can chew."

"Ah, shucks, I'm only playing a game of *Tit for Tat*," Buck answered the voice of doom.

"And which one are you?" asked the voice.

"Ah…Tat, of course!" Buck answered.

By now Dr. Kopafeel was transfigured to a vision that resembled the Venus de Milo as originally carved in marble a thousand years ago. Catching a glimpse of her breasts through the see-through negligee stirred the lust in him to a boiling point. He was close to heaven. He started to break out in a sweat.

"What and why are you staring at so pointedly?" the vision asked him with words spoken slowly as if she were speaking from the bottom of a well. "At least you didn't repeat my name when we were introduced earlier today. Otherwise, I would have slapped you across your handsome face as I have done to so many others before you."

"Slapped? Why slapped?"

"Whenever I have been introduced to a man, he repeated my name as a question and asked, "Mai I Kopafeel?"

Suddenly a blackout occurred in Buck's mind. It was a moment in time where his imagination took a bizarre twist. He recalled one of his favorite classic western films, a George Stevens production titled "Shane," photographed before the grandeur of the Grand Tetons. It was a final scene, circa 1870, between two frontier gunslingers inside Grafton's, a small-town saloon adjoining a general store.

Inside the dark pine-paneled saloon were a few tables, a long bar, and an old wood-burning stove. The lighting inside came entirely from oil lamps scattered around the rustic setting and was dim to disguise the rogues and henchmen hired to harass the settlers in the valley. Shadows that were cast on the walls everywhere made the saloon appear to be occupied by more men than actually were there.

Standing with his back against the bar and both elbows resting on top with one foot propped up on the foot rail was Buck in the role of Shane. He had his beige Stetson positioned back as far as it would go on his head. He wore a well-worn, tan calfskin jacket with leather lacing that was fringed across his chest and backside and down his sleeves. Silver medallions were evenly spaced on a wide black leather belt around his waist. In his holster was only one shiny .45 Colt revolver with ivory grips. It was the six-shooter referred to as *The Equalizer* and *the gun that won the Old Wild West*.

The expression on Buck's face personified confidence in the upcoming match of two gunslingers about to shoot it out. He now was facing not Jack Wilson, the notorious villain gunfighter from Cheyenne, but Dr. Kopafeel now dressed in a black negligee with her dark Stetson pulled down to her eyebrows and two shiny silver Colt revolvers inside their holster strapped to her hips.

Buck had never seen a body on a woman before with such perfect dimensions inside a black negligee. He had no time or room to contemplate the violence ahead. The vision of Dr. Kopafeel looked menacing to the extreme. Buck's insides melted when he saw a Sergio Leone close up of the color of her eyes: pure violet.

"I wouldn't draw if I were you, Shane," said one of the henchmen from the back of the saloon.

"So you're the gunslinger from Cheyenne," said Buck, glaring across the room.

"I wouldn't push too far if I were you," said Dr. Kopafeel, slouching in her chair.

"But you're not me," said Buck. "I heard about you."

"What have you heard?"

"I heard that you're a no-good, low-down, Yankee liar!"

There was a momentary pause as Dr. Kopafeel licked her lips and smiled. She seemed to welcome the challenge of an ensuing gunfight with this upstart juvenile.

She calmly blew on the fingers of her right hand as if to cool them down. Then she pulled each finger to crack the knuckles and covered them with a pair of tight-fitting black leather gloves. She took in a deep breath and said, "Prove it."

Finally, they both faced each other with their hands next to their six-shooters. There was an incredibly long moment of silence where you could hear a pin drop inside the saloon.

A scraggly dog suddenly rose from its rest near Buck and walked slowly across the room with its head drooping. That was one smart dog to get out of the line of fire.

Dr. Kopafeel reached for her gun to beat Buck to the draw.

But Buck was faster to aim and blasted away. The sound of gunfire reverberated off the walls as gun smoke filled the saloon.

The explosive noise in his reverie jerked Buck's head upright as he was brought back to reality. A mist had formed around him, as dense as the smoke from the shootout he had just imagined.

At this point Buck opened his eyes wider, then smiled as he caught sight of the vision of Dr. Kopafeel as she floated through a field of sunflowers and faded into the last rays of the setting sun. Buck took a deep breath and shook his head to clear his mind of any remaining lustful thoughts that had run rampant moments ago. He said to himself, "Confucius says 'Man who has sexual overtones- and undertones on park bench should be penalized for being offside with mind and groin in motion!'"

CHAPTER 10

The next morning at breakfast Marlene, Erika, and Buck were discussing their future and what to do with the reward money.

"It should be divided into thirds, that's for sure," Marlene said. "But permit me first to explain what is bouncing around in my mind. The past week has been a reawakening for me. It seems as though my mind and body have been transported into another world—one in which I found the two of you full of love. Your sincerity, tolerance, kindness, and integrity are some of the necessary attributes for a good life together. You all have given my life a new meaning. Much of it is your doing, Buck."

She paused, began to laugh at herself, then acted as though she meant to pour a glass of Chardonnay over her head; but instead she drank it in several satisfying sips. "I hereby christen myself the *Good Ship Lollypop*. Prost!"

Marlene then turned to Buck and told him, "It seems like an eternity ago when you first tromped into our lives, naked and larger than life. It is my wish and hope that you stay with us and, in time, make this your home and find a future with Erika and me here at Allesin. Living here with you has been an adventure any woman would relish for eternity. You are a credit to the whole male sex, and we are proud to have you for a friend--a good friend."

"I second your motion and emotions, Mother," said Erika. "And we now have a good reason and more than enough money to add an addition to our house."

"Well, you don't have to be a particularly religious person to feel inspired by the beauty here," said Buck. "The last week has been a roller-coaster ride that I wouldn't miss for anything in the world. Obviously, I never assumed I would be a confirmed bachelor. The perturbations in my steady heartbeat tell me that my future is here and not in Hoboken. And it is no secret that I have fallen ... what is the cliché here?... *head over heels* for your daughter."

Erika looked at Buck's face, smiled tenderly, and blew him a kiss.

"My mother always told me," said Buck, "Know yourself first and you will have insight into knowing others around you. I've been on my own since I was 11. It's true that I tried to keep two feet on the ground and bounce back up if knocked down, as my mother stressed. She was right about Fischbachau, too. It is a paradise, mostly because of people like you."

After a practical discussion about their new-found wealth, all three decided to form a revocable constructive trust to reduce the taxes on the six million euros reward from the German government for discovering and returning the Fabergé treasure trove. Marlene was unanimously elected Executor and told everyone immediately, "There will be no whining permitted anywhere, except on the farm with Trakehners who are known for a whinny or two. However, before you confirm me as Executor, there is something that both of you should know about me."

"Oh no," Erika said, "I knew it was too good to be true."

Marlene continued, "This concerns both of you, but mostly you, Buck. Something has been on my mind from the moment you discovered Max was the road bandit who stole the clothes off your back. I suspected that the bandit was Max, but I couldn't be sure. I must tell you about an incident that occurred a few years ago involving Max and me."

Marlene paused and swallowed half of the strong coffee in her cup, then continued. "Max came home unexpectedly around 3 in the afternoon—earlier than usual—and one of the farmhands was sitting at the kitchen table with nothing on but one of my dressing gowns. Max roared with rage, and tore through the house looking for me. I was in the laundry room removing the farmhand's clothes from the dryer. He had slipped and rolled down a muddy bank, and I had washed and dried his clothes.

"Max would not listen to reason. He slapped me across the face, grabbed the clothes from my hands, ran out of the house, threw the clothes in the mud, and stomped all over them. The farmhand tore out of the back door at the speed of light. I never saw him or my dressing gown again!"

"A strange bird was Max, wasn't he?" said Buck. "Maybe a cuckoo bird."

Marlene looked into Buck's eyes and continued, "When you told me about the road bandit taking your clothes, it brought back memories again of this sad incident. The big problem was we lost a good farmhand."

Erika put her arm around her mother and said with a smile, "And you lost a pretty dressing gown."

While the three were sipping their after-dinner drinks in front of the fireplace, Buck suggested that they have a celebration here at the Allesins' and invite the friends he met on the train to share their experiences in Bavaria.

Erika offered to cover the costs from the money discovered in Max's safe. "We'll invite Herr Schwartz, Herr Chipmann, and Herman and his twin boys and perhaps a neighbor or two to share our good fortune."

The three friends were feeling unbelievably happy and playful. Finally, Buck shook his head in wonderment, then telephoned Rudi Hofstedler on Marlene's cell phone to invite everyone for lunch tomorrow afternoon at the Allesins' farmhouse. Buck quickly connected with Rudi who told him the timing was perfect because everyone had returned to Winkelstüberl after attending the Oktoberfest in Munich and would be spending a few more days there.

Buck told Rudi that a car would pick up everyone, including the L'Heure twins, the following day around 11:30. He refused to give any more details so he would not spoil the fun and surprises in store for them, but he told Rudi to let everyone know that they should come prepared to regale everyone with their adventures since they had left Buck.

"Tempus Fugit!" Buck exclaimed. "It's an expression my father often used to denote 'Time flies … when you are having fun.' And I guarantee that we are going to have a lot of fun."

While Marlene was busy planning the next day's luncheon menu, the largest, oldest, most intelligent, and hairiest hog named "King Harry, the Hairy Hog" was busy with his harem unearthing some truffles near the giant oak tree. This hog had one outstanding physical identity, a band or ring around the top of his head, probably cartilage, that formed a crown, a royal crown. No one ever had the audacity to tell him that he was a royal *boar*, especially when it came to making love to his harem of gilt, a strange name for young female swine.

King Harry lifted his muddy nose high into the air, snorted, and loudly proclaimed, "Oink Oinky Oinkyoinky." In pig language, that means, "Living amid all this splendor with these gorgeous women everywhere, it's good to be the King, and I am the Truffle King!"

A statuesque porcine beauty named Countess Catrina lifted her nose and said, "King Harry doesn't need a golden crown to be a king. It is no trifle when he is in search of a truffle."

An elderly chauvinistic boar named Prince Forager poked his nose into the air and squealed, "Was all this nessa…?"

Before he could complete his words, King Harry shouted out, "Damn right, it was nessa! Think about that monk who told Marlene about the mother lode of truffles near the giant oak tree. His frock that Marlene used to cover Buck's nakedness when they first met had magical properties that passed on to Buck and eventually benefited everyone. Remember: It's good to have a frock. Everyone should have a magical frock!"

CHAPTER 11

The following day everyone was gathered in a wide circle outside the Allesins' farmhouse. They all were bursting with energy and gushing about seeing one another again. Smiles colored their faces and laughter rang throughout the afternoon. In the center were the L'Heure twins engaged in a playful exchange with the twins, Ebb and Flo, who were fawning over a small dog that Beafore L'Heure held in her arms. It was a Yorkshire terrier, cute as a button, obviously fond of Bea and Afta, and very interested in Ebb and Flo.

After the Hillstoup twins were petting the Yorkshire terrier, or Yorkie for short, Flo explained to Bea and Afta that he and Ebb were familiar with this breed of dog because their Professor of Advanced Baking at the Kochschule Berlin always brought his pet Yorkie to class to make his lessons more interesting to the students. He called it "putting a little spice into a recipe".

Ebb told them that whenever the little old Professor asked a question about a baking recipe or ingredient that stumped the class, he would point to his Yorkie -- who was sitting upright on the Professor's desk. The Yorkie would bark and motion with his front paws looking for all the world as though he knew the answer and was the world's foremost baking authority.

Flo then interjected with a big smile that the Professor would laugh and exclaim, "Jawoll! Richtig!"

"Which meant...?" asked Afta.

"Absolutely! Right!" said Ebb and Flo in unison.

Bea then told Ebb and Flo that the pet shop owner mentioned how intelligent a Yorkie was, especially after being trained to recognize signs.

Afta burst out laughing and quickly added, "But he never told us about a Yorkie's ability to answer questions about baking!"

"By the way," said Ebb, "the professor's Yorkie was named 'Muffin'!"

"Where did you find this little bundle of joy," asked Flo.

The L'Heure twins told the Hillstoup twins that they were walking to the Oktoberfest a few days ago and passed a pet shop with a sign in the window, "Free Dog for the Right Family".

"And was this the free dog?" asked Ebb, anxious for more information.

"Yes, this was the dog. Her name is Cerise. The shop owner guided us to the back of his shop," said Afta, "telling us along the way that a customer was moving into a retirement complex that prohibited animals and asked him to give the dog to a good home. He went on to tell us not to be surprised or disappointed if the dog doesn't tell you *to take her home*. That's an expression his wife uses when she sees a painting hanging in an antique store. If the painting speaks to her and tells her to *take me home*, she buys it on the spot. She managed over the years to form a high-quality collection that financed their daughter's university education."

"When the dog caught sight of us," said Beafore, "she leaped into our arms."

"She didn't have to say a word or utter a sound," said Afta. "It was love at first sight."

"Love at first sight," said Ebb, as he stroked Cerise's ears but turned his eyes toward Beafore.

"Love at first sight," said Flo, as he petted the dog's rump but turned his eyes toward Afta's rump.

A blind man could tell that sparks were flying between the twins, simply based on the choice and feelings of some simple words said between them. A few minutes later Ebb and Flo pulled their father aside and confided that they changed their plans to emigrate to America, at least for the present.

"We're ready to settle down, provided you build us a duplex on our farm," Ebb told his father, as he looked at Flo for concurrence. Flo happily nodded his assent. The boys realized that they may have met their lifetime matches in the L'Heure twins.

"We'll pay you back from profits on our catering business," said Flo.

Ebb continued, "For a model of our catering business we plan on using the noted 'Feincost Käfer' of Prinzeregentenstrasse in Munich."

A few minutes later everyone was seated outside around a wide circular table. Marlene told the friends Buck had met on the train about her plans to construct an indoor arena for handicapped riders who would benefit from therapeutic riding.

Marlene mentioned a second venture involving truffles. She planned to sell the truffles discovered by the truffle hogs, who would unearth truffles where Schwartz discovered them in the woods. The pigs had a good sense of smell and were able to identify truffles buried as deep as three feet underground. The pigs for Marlene and Schwartz's project only had to dig less than one foot.

Marlene told everyone, "This venture could be a money maker from the get go, according to Detective Schwartz who has just retired again and is soon to become my partner."

She then pointed in the direction of the giant Oak tree and said, "I ask you all now to swear that you will not disclose the location of the mother lode of truffles. We will choose the right time to tell the world that this area was first discovered by a monk from Kloster Maxlrain who blessed it and proclaimed it the mother lode of truffles. We will use 'The Mother Lode of Truffles' on the logo on our containers and shipping labels."

Next up, Erika told them about her plans to resurrect the music of Bert Klemperer from the 1950s. "I grew up listening to the audio cassettes that were left by the farmhouse's previous owner. Klemperer's arrangements are priceless and should be marketed to millions of lovers of music of the '50s, not only in Germany but in America, France, Italy, and around the world. His star of popularity has slipped temporarily under a cloud, but I am willing to put my energy and money to send it ascending again. I plan on purchasing the estate as a treasured intellectual literary property, then hire an arranger and conductor to form a partnership with me."

"That is the perfect thing for you to do, meine Liebe!" Buck exclaimed and then blushed when he realized he had used the German phrase for "my Sweetheart".

Marlene smiled inwardly and then covered Buck's blushing by asking everyone to lift their steins in a toast to the American visitors who had made their first visit to Fischbachau. "May they have a long and fruitful life of joy and happiness, and may they remember that kindness will make their dreams come true."

Erika then said directly to the travelers, "Before turning over the floor, in this case the ground here in Fischbachau, to Buck my mother and I would like to get to know you all better, and I'm sure Buck wants to hear all about your Oktoberfest adventures. So let's go around the table and have you tell us about your recent adventures in Bavaria."

The L'Heure twins were the first to rise and began to speak as if they were Siamese twins, with one starting a sentence or idea and the other finishing it or adding to it.

Bea started off by telling them, "We couldn't wait to see our private workspace at the academy and meet our professor, Frau Emma von Piloty, the great granddaughter of the former director Karl von Piloty. She could not have been more accommodating and considerate."

Afta chimed in, "Professor von Piloty suggested, correction recommended, that we promptly pay a visit to a bakery in Schwabing that is close to the academy and talk to the owner whose daughter was recently married and moved to another town. If we played our cards right, she told us, there might be a possibility of renting the daughter's room above the bakery and paying for it by giving him a painting each month."

Bea told them, "We rushed to the bakery and the Professor was right about everything she told us. The owner looked to be in his late 60s…"

"His name is Okeydokey Szakall," said Afta. "We call him 'Okey bácsi' – that's Hungarian for Uncle Okey. He told us how much he missed his daughter and her friends who came to visit. He told us how he loved his horses when he rode them on the Puszta plains of Hungary as a youngster. We agreed to give him a painting a month in exchange for room and board."

"There were tears in his eyes," said Bea, "as he escorted us to his daughter's room above the bakery and spoke about the love he had for her. He begged us to stay, welcoming us and inviting us to be a part of his family."

"He promised us to do everything humanly possible to make our stay in Munich memorable, one that would provide memories for a lifetime," Afta added.

"By the way," concluded Bea, "the smell of freshly baked croissants and a Hungarian specialty of onion, garlic, and cheese sprinkled on a Swedish type flat bun made our mouths water while he was talking. It was heavenly. He mentioned that his wife was the best cook whose specialty was Hungarian goulash and potato pancakes."

"I hope you will try to watch your figures and the calories," said Flo.

"You can bet the farm that we will be watching your figures," said Ebb softly.

"Wunderbar," said all the twins in unison.

Marlene said, "The first days of your life in Bavaria clearly show the friendly nature and kindness of the German people."

"Speaking of friendliness," chimed in Buck, "let's hear from our husband and wife from Philadelphia, the city of brotherly love."

Rudi rose and told them, "As Al Jolson said a long time ago, 'You ain't heard nothin' yet.' Inside one of the tents at the Oktoberfest, after we finished our heavenly dish of sweinsaxe, kosher pork baked in a wine sauce, and swallowed half of a stein of beer, Sylvia joined with hundreds of happy but slightly tipsy customers in singing an old but still popular ballad titled 'You Can't Be True Dear.' My wife sang it first in German, loud enough for the waiter to notice her. The waiter told the band leader about Sylvia's voice. During a brief intermission, the band leader asked her to sing it again with the band on stage and the rest is history. She was an immediate hit. Give them a sampling, meine Schatze."

Immediately upon hearing her name called out, the dog Schatze's ears shot upward as Sylvia was thrilled to sing the song again for her friends. She told them that the music was composed by Hans Otten with German lyrics by Gerhard Ebeler and English lyrics by Hal Cotton. Sylvia was preparing to sing when Herman begged them to wait a minute. He disappeared for two minutes then returned with a huge grin and a pearl inlaid Horner accordion he had retrieved from his car.

Sylvia began to sing, accompanied by Herman on his accordion.

Schatze "sang" along with Sylvia until Buck raised his finger to his lips and motioned Schatze to be quiet.

> *You can't be true dear, there's nothing more to say, I*
> *trusted you dear, hoping we'd find a way*
> *Your kisses tell me that you and I are through*
> *But I'll keep loving you, although you can't be true.*
>
> *Clouds hide the sun in the skies that were blue*
> *As my heart says farewell to the joy that I knew*

Love, to be real, is a love to be shared
But I know that you never cared.
Song: You Can't Be True, Dear lyrics - Patti Page

"Afterward," Rudi continued, "the band leader, and a representative of the brewery sponsoring his band, offered us one month free in a fully-furnished apartment on the condition that Sylvia sing two songs a night for the two-week Oktoberfest next year."

"They particularly liked my rendition of 'We'll Meet Again, Don't Know Where, Don't Know When' to close out each evening of the 'fest," said Sylvia. "It's a ballad composed by Ross Parker with lyrics by Hughie Charles."

"This would be a good way to end our visit here with you," said Rudi. "Sing it like Vera Lynn did in the 1940s, meine Schatze."

"I love being called Schatze," said Sylvia, "I'm glad to know I am your Darling. I hope you like this song as much as I do. If you know it, sing along with me, please."

"But that does not mean you, meine Kleine Schatze," laughed Buck pointing at the canine Schatze who once again had reacted to hearing her name.

Ignoring Buck's admonition, Schatze once again began to "sing" in her dog's voice in harmony with Sylvia. This time Buck shrugged his shoulders with a grin and let her join in because she seemed to enjoy it so much. It was a touching moment right out of a Walt Disney film when Sylvia began singing as tears slowly formed in her eyes.

We'll meet again, don't know where, don't know when
But I know we'll meet again some sunny day
Keep smiling through, just like you always do
'Till the blue skies drive the dark clouds far away.
So, will you please say hello, to the folks that I know
Tell them I won't be long, they'll be happy to know

That as you saw me go, I was singing this song.
We'll meet again, don't know where, don't know when
Song: We'll Meet Again - Vera Lynn

After everyone gave Sylvia a standing ovation, Marlene swallowed a good portion of Maxlrain beer and took a deep breath. "Now is the time to put the spotlight on someone you thought you knew from your travels with him, someone who finally found the birthplace of his mother, the home that she grew up in, and Fischbachau, the place she called a paradise."

Finally, Buck, who had waited patiently for this opportunity, rose in slow motion, then took a deep breath, removed his signature sunglasses and Stetson, smiled the biggest of smiles and gave a snappy salute. ***"Have I got a story for you!"***

THE END ...
... or is it?

Stay tuned for the upcoming sequels, titled:

Freelance – Give me the Concierge

Freelance – Send in the Clowns

Cast Of Characters

Buck Simon Brightman

An occasionally brash 29-year old American who left a job in corporate marketing to pursue a career in his first love, photojournalism. Now he was making his first trip outside the USA in search of his mother's birthplace in a small village in Bavaria, Germany. His pronounced characteristics include the western Stetson and Porsche Aviator sunglasses that he rarely removed. He rarely said "Goodbye," preferring instead to give a snappy salute, an act of homage to his father, a career officer in the U. S. Marine Corps.

May Bea Furshore

A sexy farmer's daughter who had a brief encounter with Buck in the corridor of an ICE train from Stuttgart to Munich.

Max Allesin

A complex 50-year old brute whose physique resembled a pro wrestler. He was a Bavarian farmer and veterinarian who specialized in the breeding of Trakehners with Arabian bloodlines but was obsessed with the profit to be made by inserting a computer chip into the mane of certain horses exported to an ISIS agent in Saudi Arabia. He was paranoid and suspected he was being spied on. He was also a tortured soul, with delusions of superiority in a picturesque Bavarian village 37 miles outside Munich called Fischbachau. He may have approached the doorstep of insanity because of concussions from several falls. He hated Jews and was abusive to everyone around him, especially to his family.

Marlene Allesin

Max's wife who married him at age 23 after graduating from law school. She was now 45 years old but looked five years younger. A beautiful and intelligent woman of small stature who has realized that she may have wasted her married life with Max, except for the birth of her daughter.

Erika Allesin

Max and Marlene's attractive and intelligent daughter, now 21; tall and slim. Only high school educated but much brighter and logical than others of her age. She took abuse from her father and was always able to bounce back stronger than before.

Rudi Hofstedler

A 50-year old, much sought-after trust attorney with connections to the movers and shakers of Philadelphia.

Sylvia Hofstedler

Rudi's wife, 45; married for 20 years, and blessed with a marvelous speaking and singing voice.

Beafore L'Heure

A gifted, sexy 21-year-old French twin from New Orleans.

Afta L'Heure

Beafore's twin sister, born one hour later.

Khalid "Cal" Najjar Khalid

(Khalid means eternal or immortal or everlasting. Najjar means Carpenter, ironically the occupation of Jesus's earthly father). Khalid was the third child and oldest son of Yemeni parents. He was a successful business man who first exported high-quality coffee from Yemen and later became an ISIS agent who recruited farmers in Bavaria to participate in a student exchange program. Cal, as he liked to be called, hired Max and together they exported Max's cross-bred Trakehners to a horse trainer for the Saudi Royal Family. Unbeknownst to the Saudi Royal Family, the trainer was an active member of ISIS.

Haim Fugit

A bus driver and owner of Haim Transit; self-proclaimed poet laureate.

Herman Hillstoup

A farmer and widower whose farm was next to Marlene's. He crossbred cows, a technology that Max pirated and modified for breeding his Trakehners.

Ebenezer "Ebb" Hillstoup

A 27-year-old, first-born twin son of Herman Hillstoup. Bright and ambitious chef.

Florenz "Flo" Hillstoup

The brother of Ebb, born 30 minutes after his brother. Equal in all ways to his brother. Together they can start and finish a sentence without a pause or missing a beat.

Tutz Suite

The owner of rental bicycle shop in Fischbachau.

Felix Chipmann

The Head of the Homicide of the Federal Criminal Police Bureau of rural Bavaria, known as *Bundeskriminalamt,* abbreviated BKA.

Ernst Rolf Schwartz

The Chief of Detectives working under Chipmann. A brilliant forensic investigator with a fine record of 25 years of experience with the BKA.

Franz Funk

The grandson of Reich Minister of Economics Walther Funk who could never forgive the German people for not supporting Hitler. Now a 90-year-old respected farmer who entered into a student exchange program that he did not know was a plot to plant two students under ISIS command for terrorist acts against Germany.

Ali Mohammed Shiptoshur

An exchange student and ISIS trainee sent to a Bavarian farmer as an exchange student to learn the latest technology in the production of hops. The exchange program was, at its heart and unbeknownst to the Bavarian farmers who participated in it, a front for future ISIS terrorist acts.

Ben Ladeen

An exchange student with the same responsibility as Ali, except for his being radicalized in Iran and beyond hope of being deradicalized.

I Fagotta (aka "Izzy")

An interrogator in Internal Affairs, Munich Bureau BKA.

Okeydokey Szakall

A chubby, renowned Hungarian baker who owned the best bakery in Schwabing, the university area of Munich, and who gave lodging to the L'Heure twins. The twins affectionately refer to him as "Okey bácsi", which is Hungarian for Uncle Okey.

Dr. Mai I. Kopafeel

A 28-year-old blond bombshell with a Ph.D. in Antiquities; curator of historic treasures in the Grünes Gewölbe (Green Vault), Dresden. Noted German expert and author of "Faberge Eggs – More Profound; Never Round".

Schatze

A lovable female Golden Retriever who was more than a pet to the Allesin family (and who saved Buck's dignity).

Moxie

Herman Hillstoup's best friend, a 12-year old German Short-Haired Pointer.

Harry the Hog

The largest and hairiest wild hog who uncovered the mother lode of truffles near a giant oak tree in the woods on the Allesin farm.

Cerise (French for Cherry)

A young, very intelligent Yorkie (Yorkshire Terrier), born in England and given to the L'Heure twins by the owner of a pet shop across from Olympia Park, where the Oktoberfest is held.

Muffin

A Yorkie with considerable knowledge of baking (or so it would appear) who belonged to Ebb and Flo's Professor of Advanced Baking at the Kochschule Berlin.

Addendum

List of Paintings

Photographs of art displayed in this book are from the collection of the author. Each work's title (with English translation where needed), artist, medium, and size is given below.

"Der Hintersee mit dem Hoher Göll" – "The Hintersee with the Hoher Göll" by Josef Thoma, the Younger (German 1828-1899). Painting, 38" x 56".

"Cheval Demi-Sang" (Tête Levée) – "Half-Blood Horse with Head Raised" by Antoine Louis Barye (French 1795-1875). Bronze, 5" high.

"The Reading Lesson" by Ludwig Vollmar (German1842-1884). Painting, 32" x 37".

"Arab Horsemen in a Mountainous Landscape" – by Adolf Schreyer (German 1828-1899). Painting, 23.75" x 31.5"

"Ruby" by Edmund Osthaus (German–American 1858-1928). Watercolor on paper, 5" x 7".

"Frühlings am Fang Starnberger See" – "Springtime Fishing at Starnberger Lake" by Otto Pippel (German 1878-1960). Painting, 42" x 38".